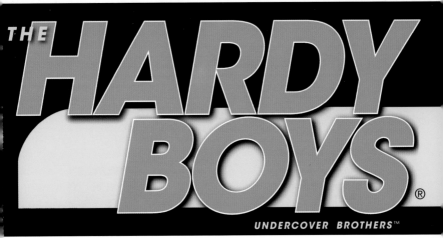

THE HARDY BOYS

BOYS

UNDERCOVER BROTHERS™

PAPERCUTZ

THE HARDY BOYS®

THE HARDY BOYS

UNDERCOVER BROTHERS™

#1

The Ocean of Osyria

SCOTT LOBDELL • Writer
LEA HERNANDEZ • Artist
preview art by DANIEL RENDON
Based on the series by
FRANKLIN W. DIXON

New York

The Ocean of Oysyria
SCOTT LOBDELL – Writer
LEA HERNANDEZ — Artist
BRYAN SENKA – Letterer
LOVERN KINDZIERSKI — Colorists
JIM SALICRUP
Editor-in-Chief

ISBN-10: 1-59707-001-7 paperback edition
ISBN-13: 1-59707-001-0 paperback edition
ISBN-10: 1-59707-005-X hardcover edition
ISBN-13: 1-59707-005-8 hardcover edition

10   9   8   7   6   5   4   3   2

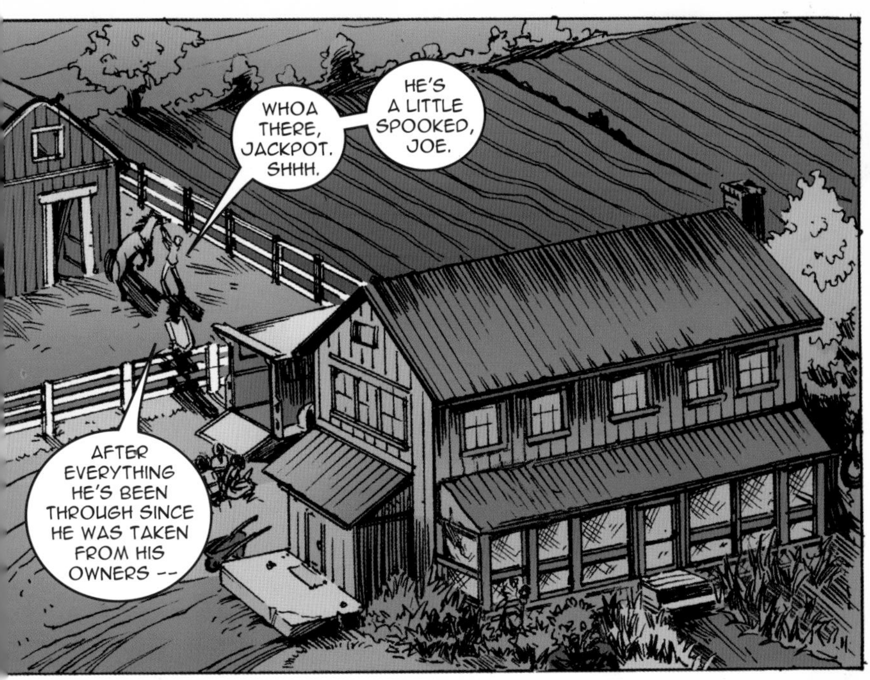
WHOA THERE, JACKPOT. SHHH.
HE'S A LITTLE SPOOKED, JOE.
AFTER EVERYTHING HE'S BEEN THROUGH SINCE HE WAS TAKEN FROM HIS OWNERS --

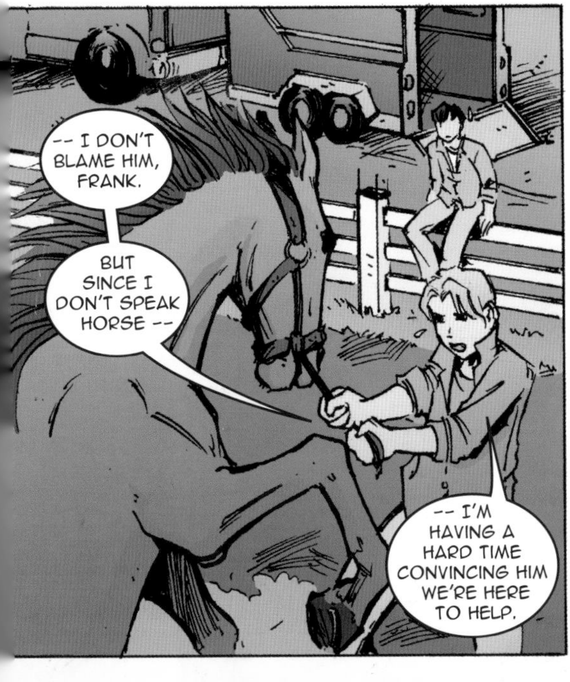
-- I DON'T BLAME HIM, FRANK.
BUT SINCE I DON'T SPEAK HORSE --
-- I'M HAVING A HARD TIME CONVINCING HIM WE'RE HERE TO HELP.

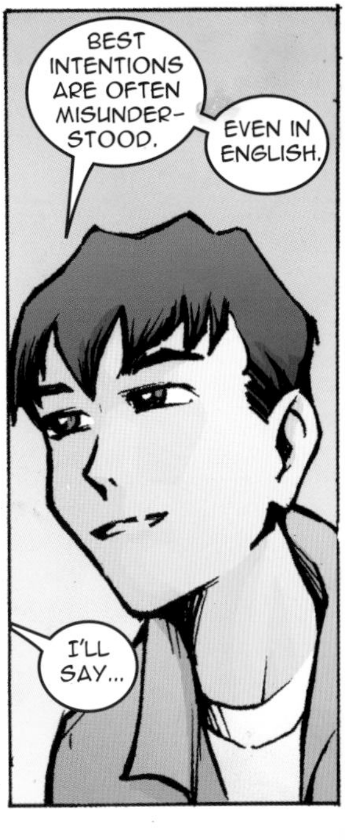
BEST INTENTIONS ARE OFTEN MISUNDER-STOOD.
EVEN IN ENGLISH.
I'LL SAY...

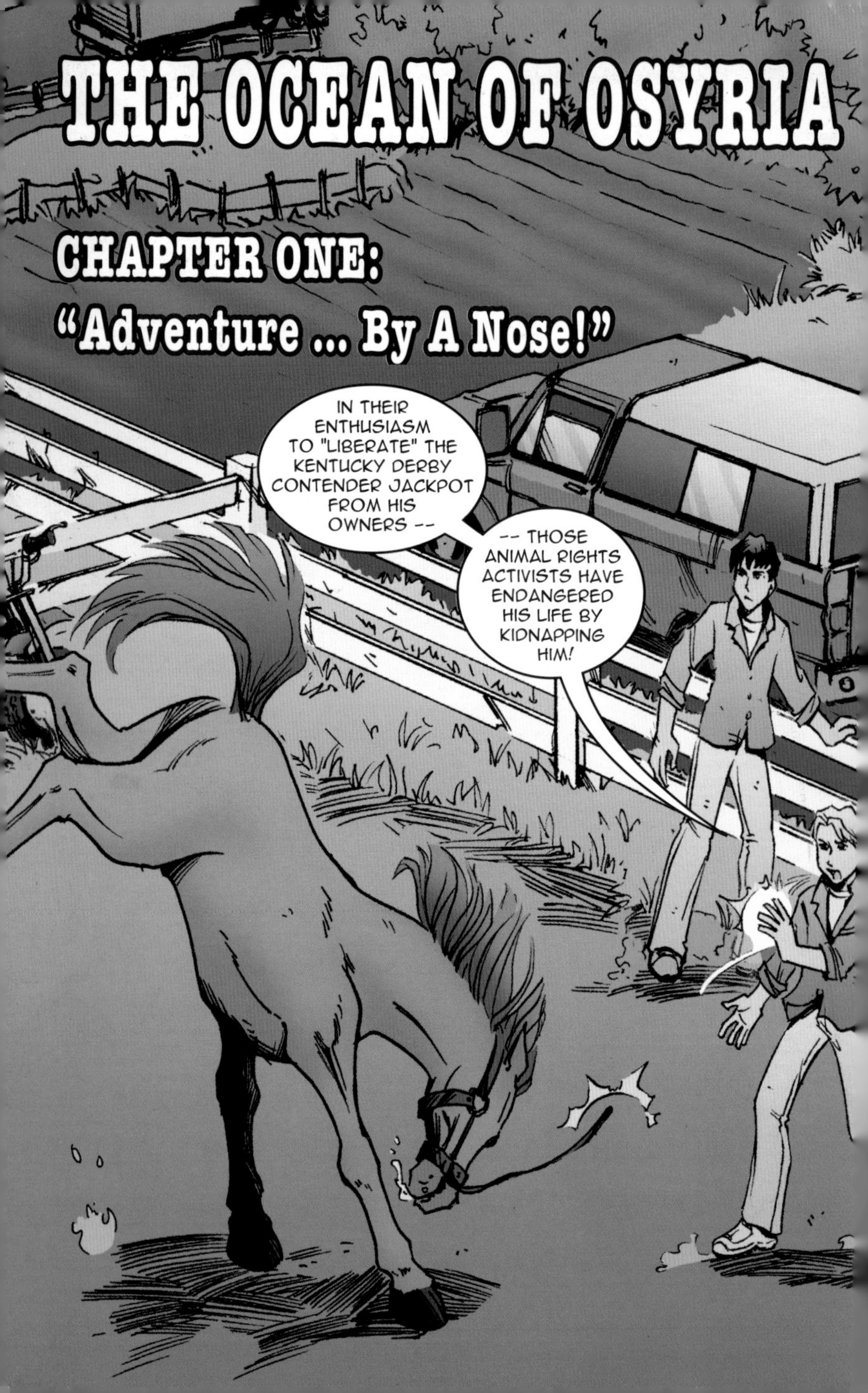
THE OCEAN OF OSYRIA
CHAPTER ONE:
"Adventure ... By A Nose!"
IN THEIR ENTHUSIASM TO "LIBERATE" THE KENTUCKY DERBY CONTENDER JACKPOT FROM HIS OWNERS --
-- THOSE ANIMAL RIGHTS ACTIVISTS HAVE ENDANGERED HIS LIFE BY KIDNAPPING HIM!

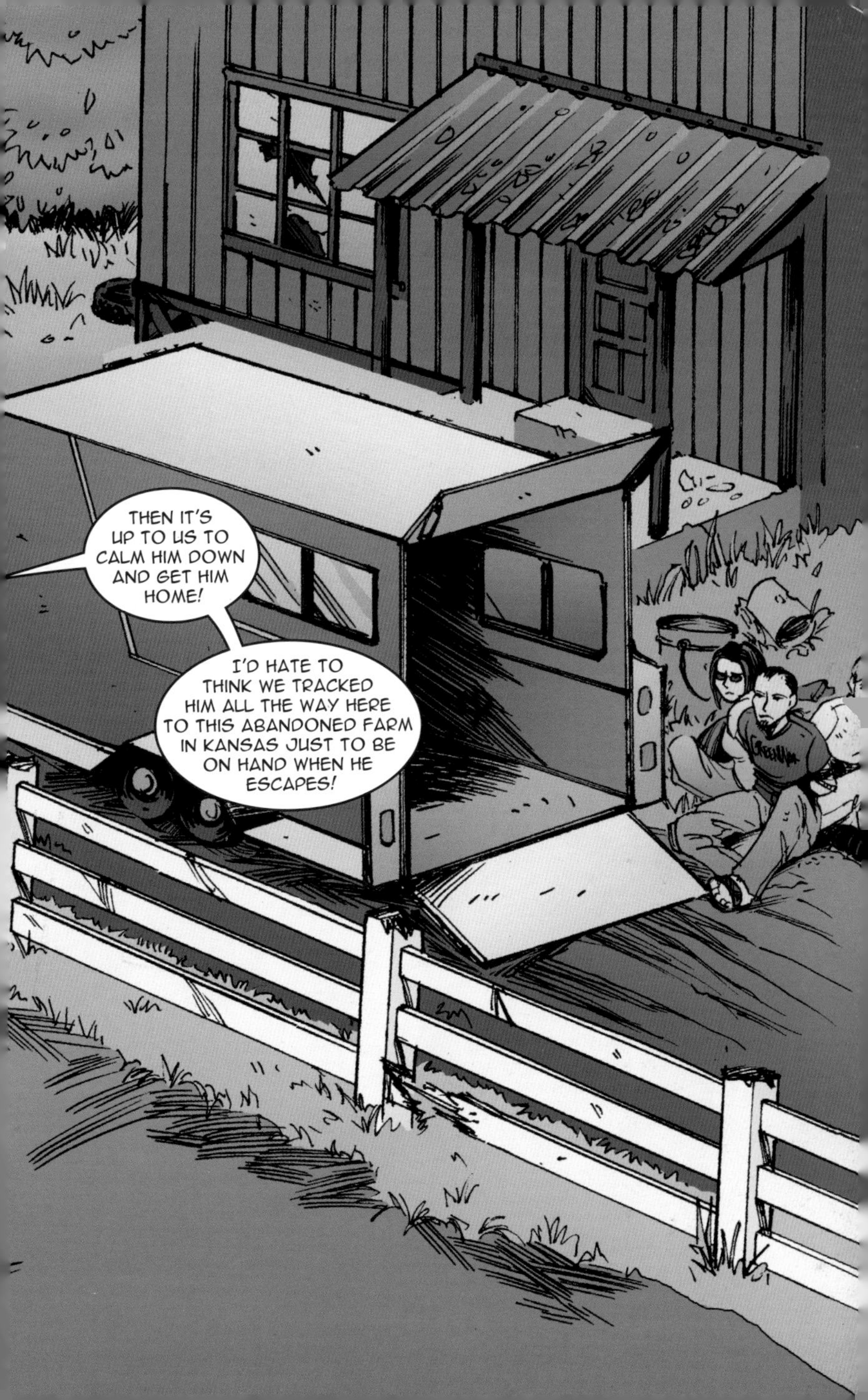
THEN IT'S UP TO US TO CALM HIM DOWN AND GET HIM HOME!
I'D HATE TO THINK WE TRACKED HIM ALL THE WAY HERE TO THIS ABANDONED FARM IN KANSAS JUST TO BE ON HAND WHEN HE ESCAPES!

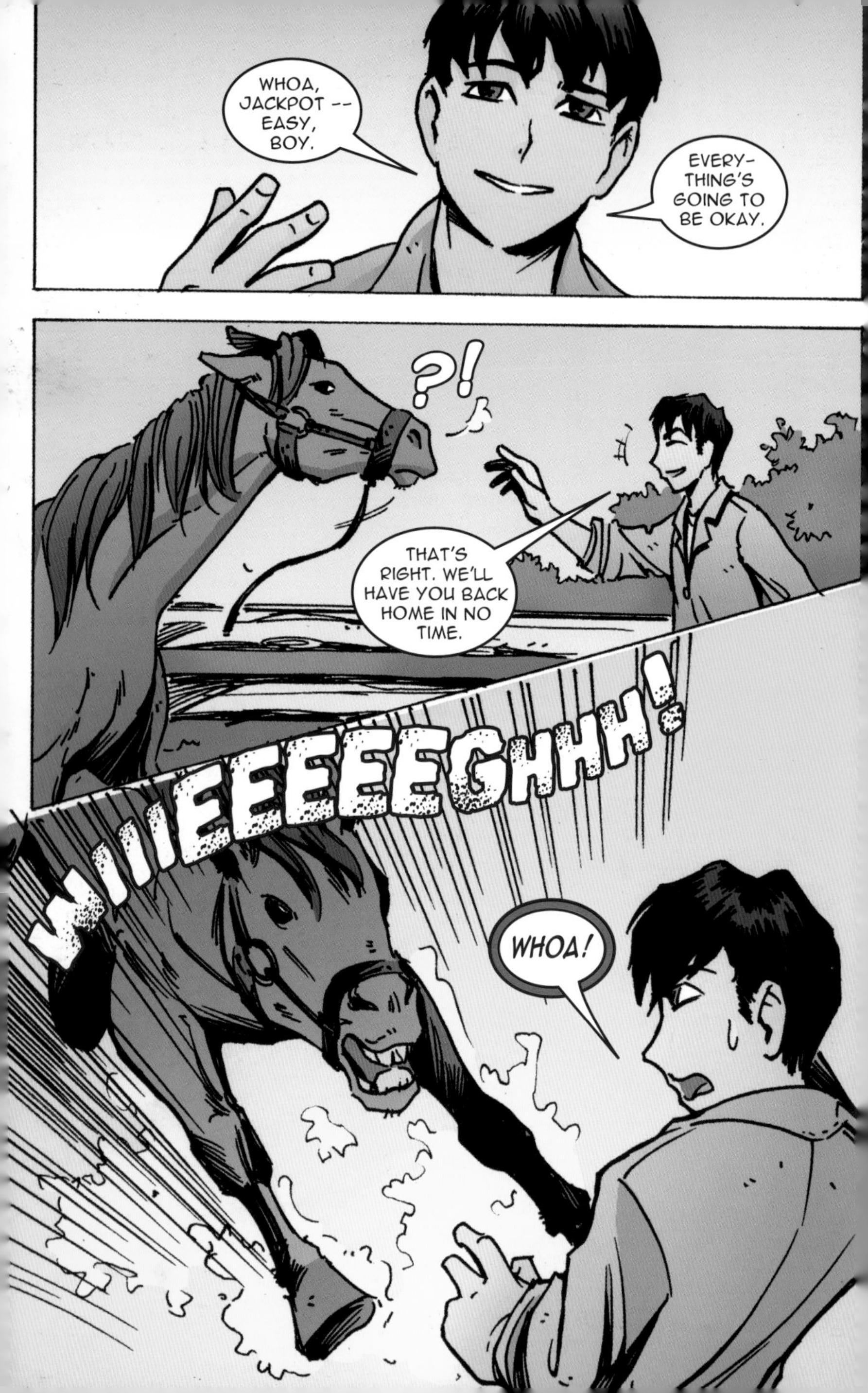
WHOA, JACKPOT -- EASY, BOY.
EVERY-THING'S GOING TO BE OKAY.
?!
THAT'S RIGHT. WE'LL HAVE YOU BACK HOME IN NO TIME.
WHIIIEEEEEEGHHH!
WHOA!

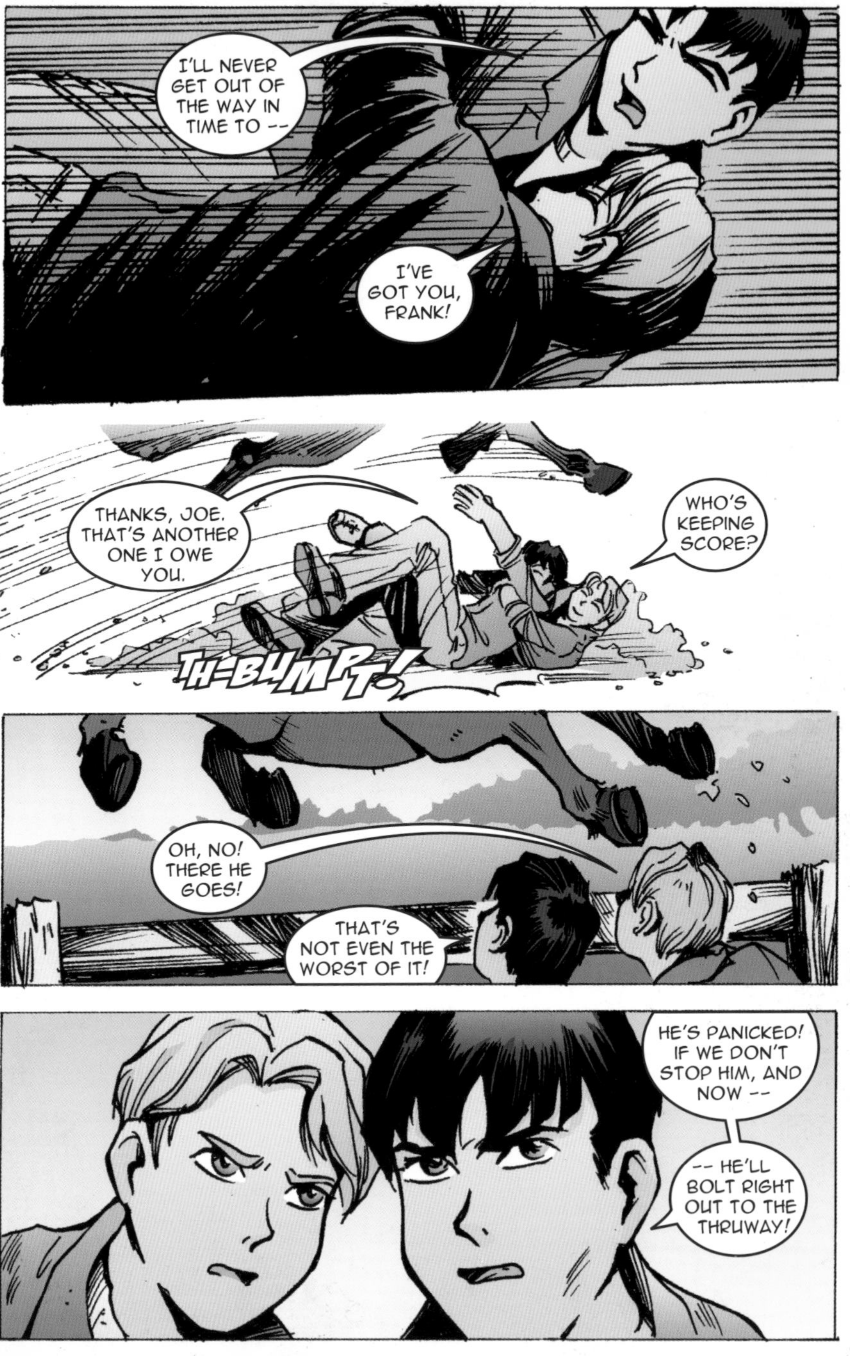
I'LL NEVER GET OUT OF THE WAY IN TIME TO --
I'VE GOT YOU, FRANK!
THANKS, JOE. THAT'S ANOTHER ONE I OWE YOU.
WHO'S KEEPING SCORE?
TH-BUMPT!
OH, NO! THERE HE GOES!
THAT'S NOT EVEN THE WORST OF IT!
HE'S PANICKED! IF WE DON'T STOP HIM, AND NOW --
-- HE'LL BOLT RIGHT OUT TO THE THRUWAY!

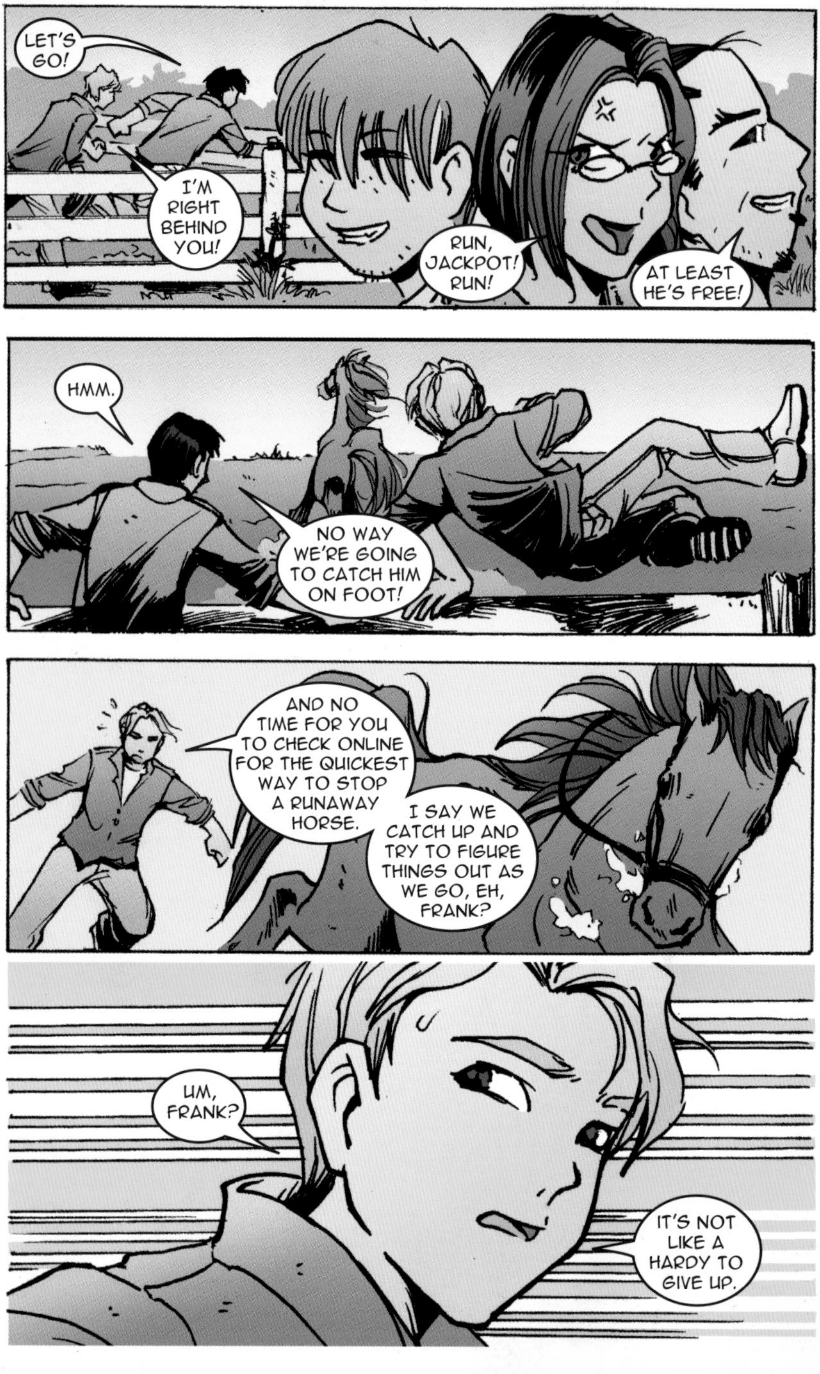
LET'S GO!
I'M RIGHT BEHIND YOU!
RUN, JACKPOT! RUN!
AT LEAST HE'S FREE!
HMM.
NO WAY WE'RE GOING TO CATCH HIM ON FOOT!
AND NO TIME FOR YOU TO CHECK ONLINE FOR THE QUICKEST WAY TO STOP A RUNAWAY HORSE.
I SAY WE CATCH UP AND TRY TO FIGURE THINGS OUT AS WE GO, EH, FRANK?
UM, FRANK?
IT'S NOT LIKE A HARDY TO GIVE UP.

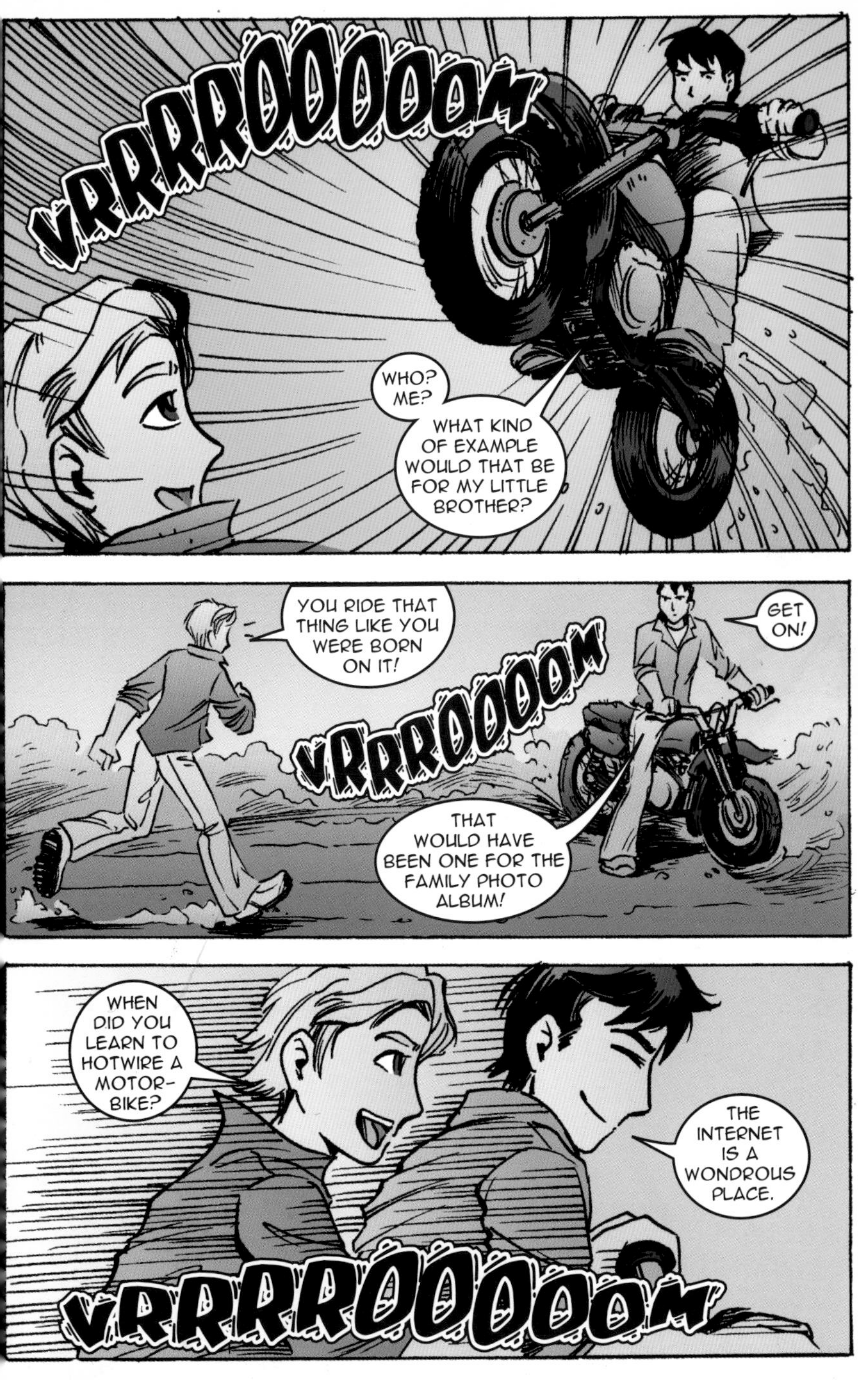
VRRRROOOOOOM
WHO? ME?
WHAT KIND OF EXAMPLE WOULD THAT BE FOR MY LITTLE BROTHER?
YOU RIDE THAT THING LIKE YOU WERE BORN ON IT!
GET ON!
VRRROOOOOM
THAT WOULD HAVE BEEN ONE FOR THE FAMILY PHOTO ALBUM!
WHEN DID YOU LEARN TO HOTWIRE A MOTOR-BIKE?
THE INTERNET IS A WONDROUS PLACE.
VRRRROOOOOOOM

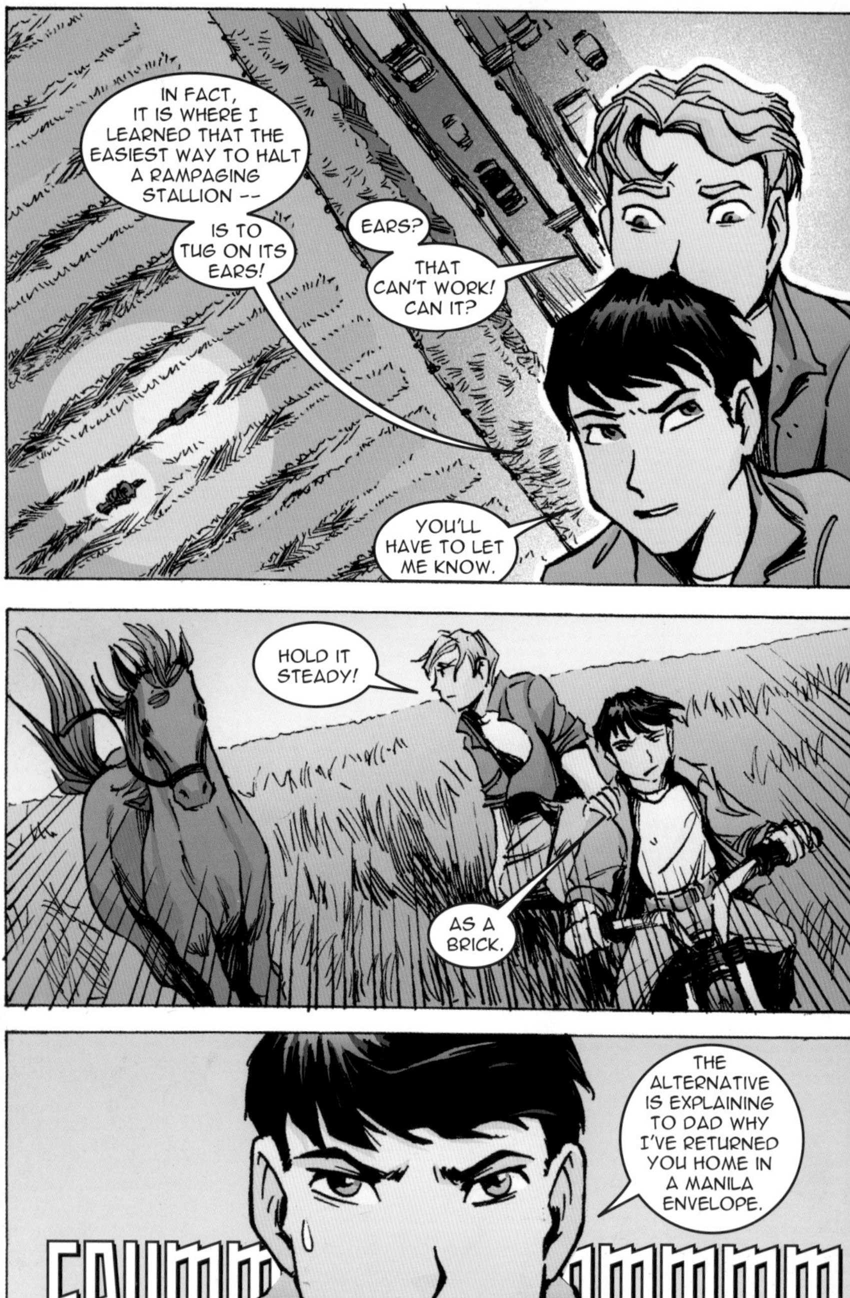
IN FACT, IT IS WHERE I LEARNED THAT THE EASIEST WAY TO HALT A RAMPAGING STALLION --
IS TO TUG ON ITS EARS!
EARS?
THAT CAN'T WORK! CAN IT?
YOU'LL HAVE TO LET ME KNOW.
HOLD IT STEADY!
AS A BRICK.
THE ALTERNATIVE IS EXPLAINING TO DAD WHY I'VE RETURNED YOU HOME IN A MANILA ENVELOPE.
FRUMMMMMMMM

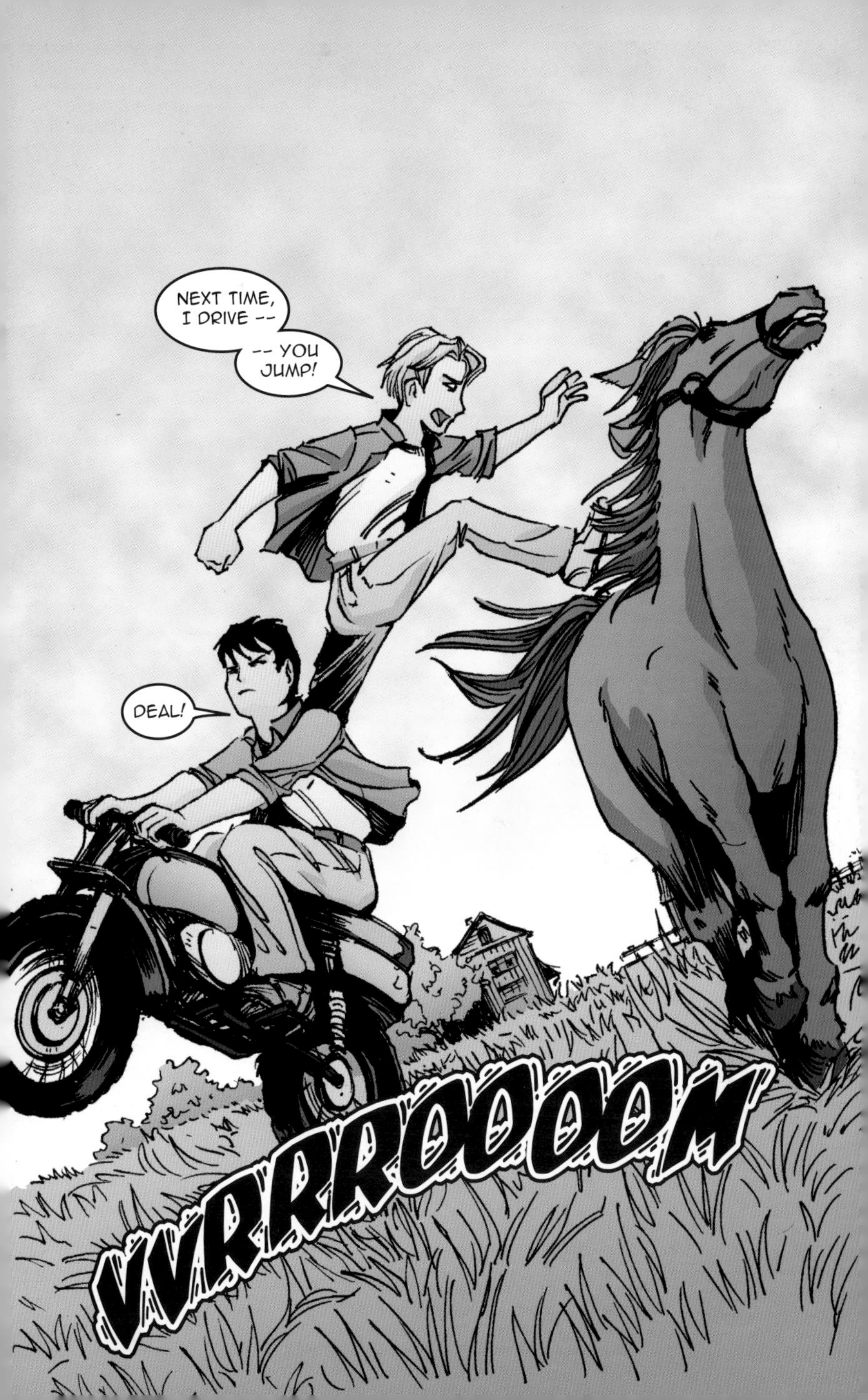
NEXT TIME, I DRIVE --
-- YOU JUMP!
DEAL!
VVRRROOOOM

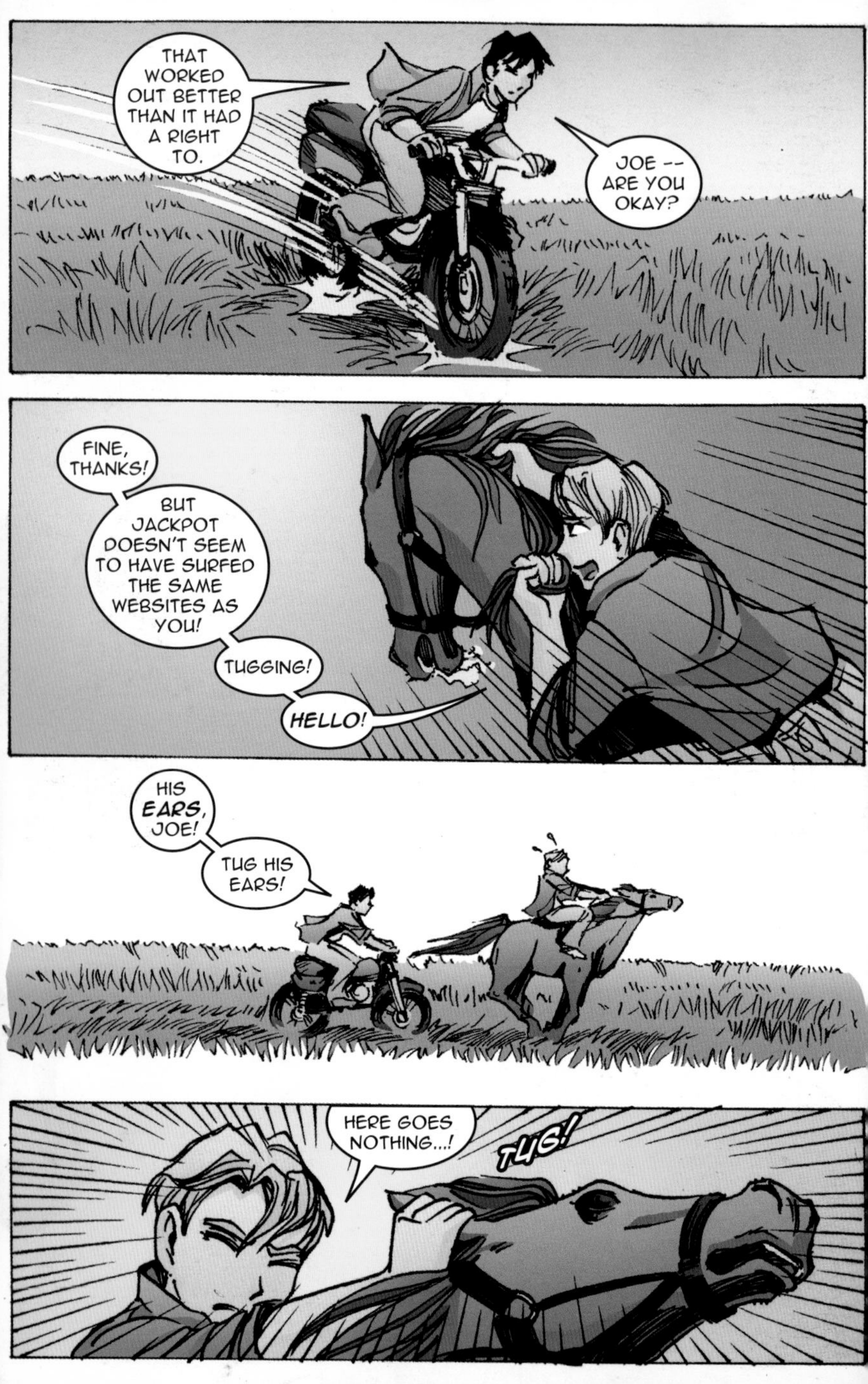
THAT WORKED OUT BETTER THAN IT HAD A RIGHT TO.
JOE -- ARE YOU OKAY?
FINE, THANKS!
BUT JACKPOT DOESN'T SEEM TO HAVE SURFED THE SAME WEBSITES AS YOU!
TUGGING!
HELLO!
HIS EARS, JOE!
TUG HIS EARS!
HERE GOES NOTHING...!
TUG!

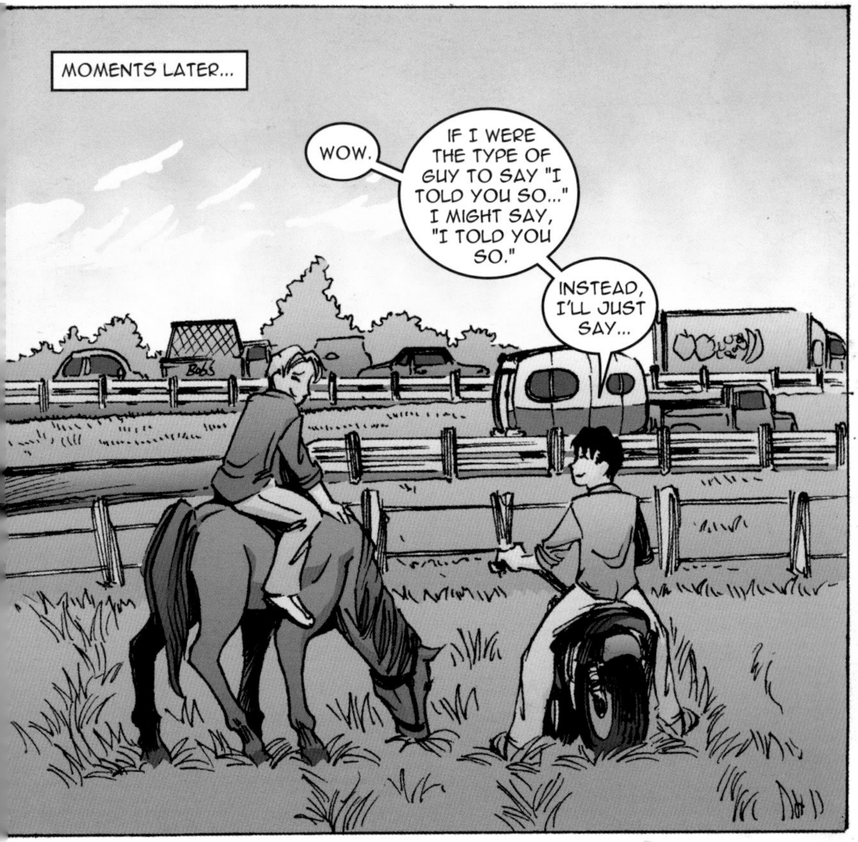
MOMENTS LATER...
WOW.
IF I WERE THE TYPE OF GUY TO SAY "I TOLD YOU SO..." I MIGHT SAY, "I TOLD YOU SO."
INSTEAD, I'LL JUST SAY...
Bobs

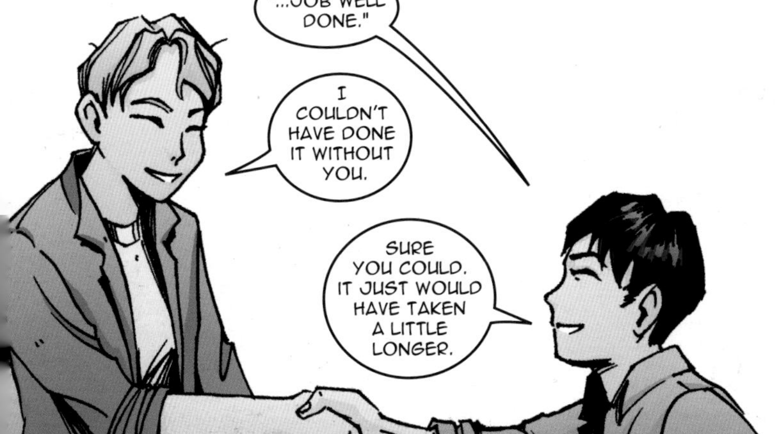
"...JOB WELL DONE."
I COULDN'T HAVE DONE IT WITHOUT YOU.
SURE YOU COULD. IT JUST WOULD HAVE TAKEN A LITTLE LONGER.

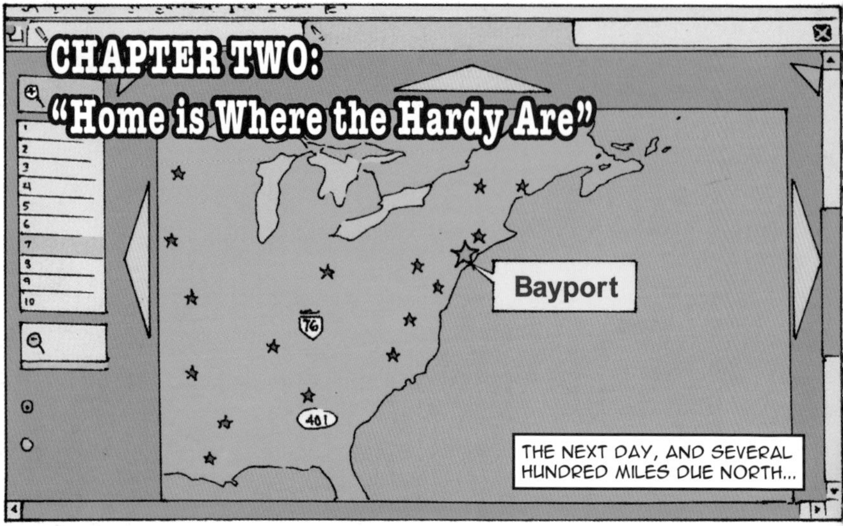
CHAPTER TWO:
"Home is Where the Hardy Are"
Bayport
76
481
THE NEXT DAY, AND SEVERAL HUNDRED MILES DUE NORTH...

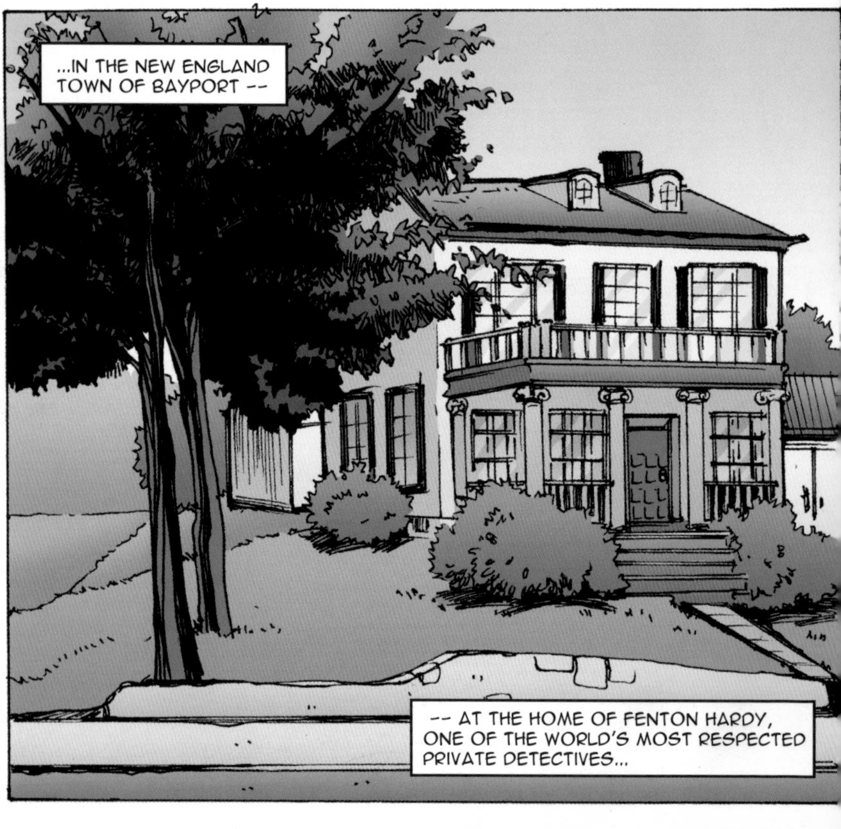
...IN THE NEW ENGLAND TOWN OF BAYPORT --
-- AT THE HOME OF FENTON HARDY, ONE OF THE WORLD'S MOST RESPECTED PRIVATE DETECTIVES...

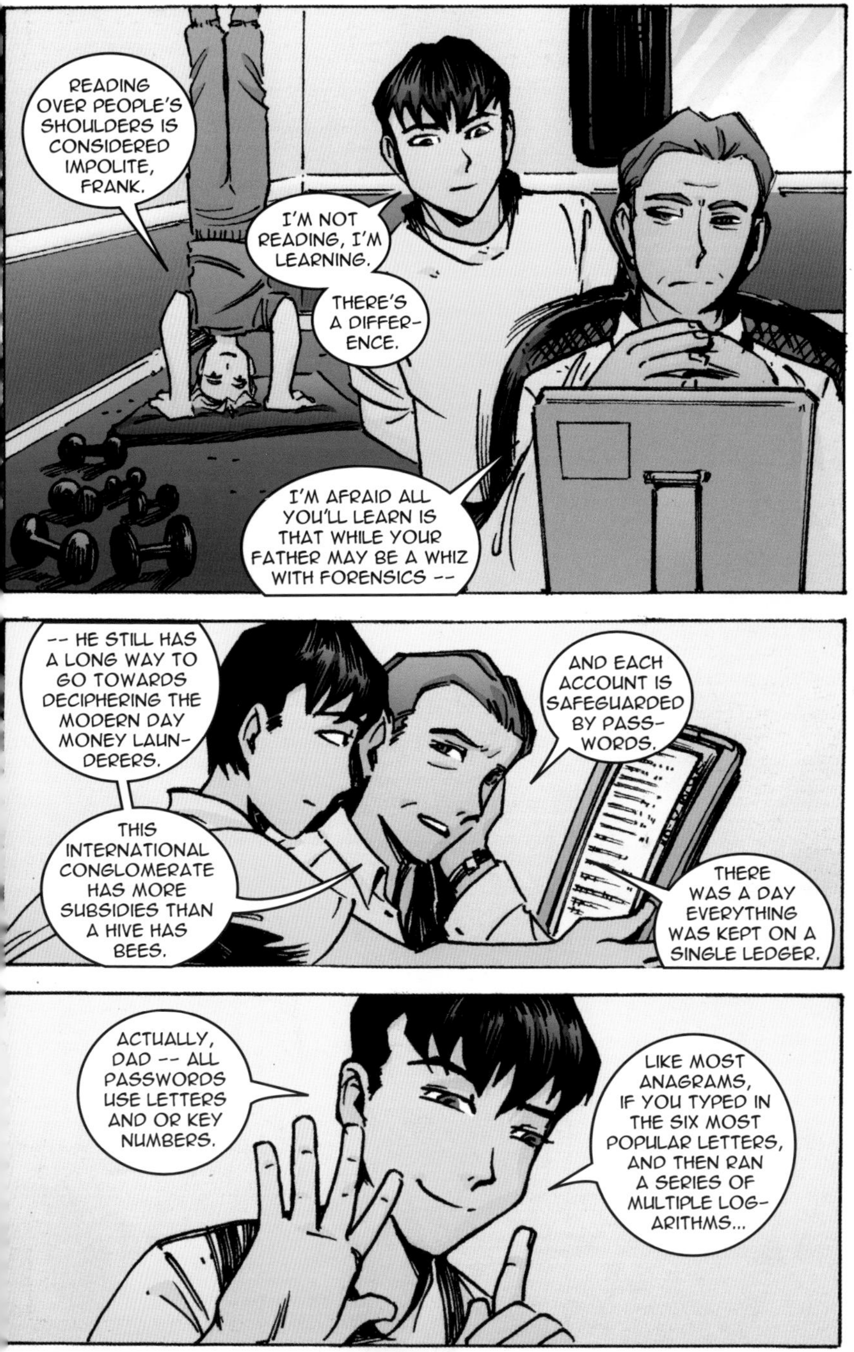
READING OVER PEOPLE'S SHOULDERS IS CONSIDERED IMPOLITE, FRANK.
I'M NOT READING, I'M LEARNING.
THERE'S A DIFFERENCE.
I'M AFRAID ALL YOU'LL LEARN IS THAT WHILE YOUR FATHER MAY BE A WHIZ WITH FORENSICS --
-- HE STILL HAS A LONG WAY TO GO TOWARDS DECIPHERING THE MODERN DAY MONEY LAUNDERERS.
THIS INTERNATIONAL CONGLOMERATE HAS MORE SUBSIDIES THAN A HIVE HAS BEES.
AND EACH ACCOUNT IS SAFEGUARDED BY PASSWORDS.
THERE WAS A DAY EVERYTHING WAS KEPT ON A SINGLE LEDGER.
ACTUALLY, DAD -- ALL PASSWORDS USE LETTERS AND OR KEY NUMBERS.
LIKE MOST ANAGRAMS, IF YOU TYPED IN THE SIX MOST POPULAR LETTERS, AND THEN RAN A SERIES OF MULTIPLE LOGARITHMS...

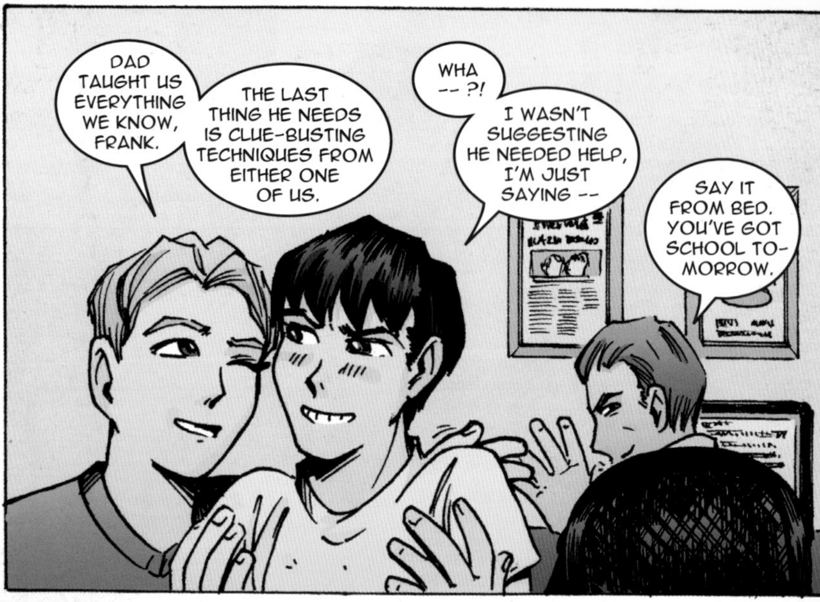
DAD TAUGHT US EVERYTHING WE KNOW, FRANK.
THE LAST THING HE NEEDS IS CLUE-BUSTING TECHNIQUES FROM EITHER ONE OF US.
WHA -- ?!
I WASN'T SUGGESTING HE NEEDED HELP, I'M JUST SAYING --
SAY IT FROM BED. YOU'VE GOT SCHOOL TO-MORROW.
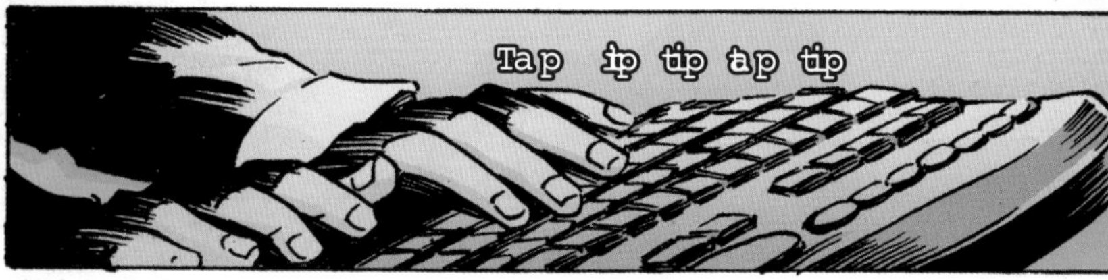
Tap tip tip tap tip
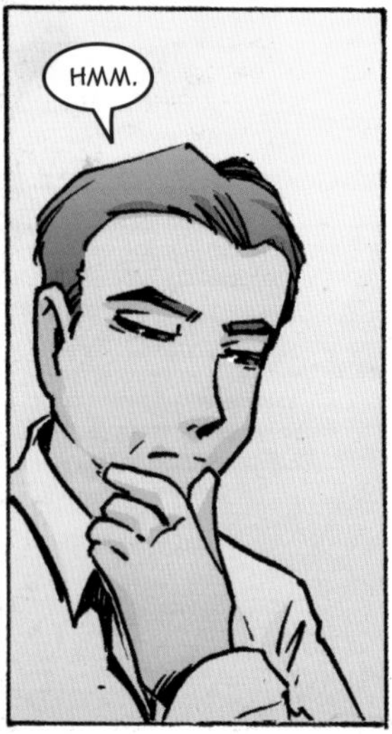
HMM.
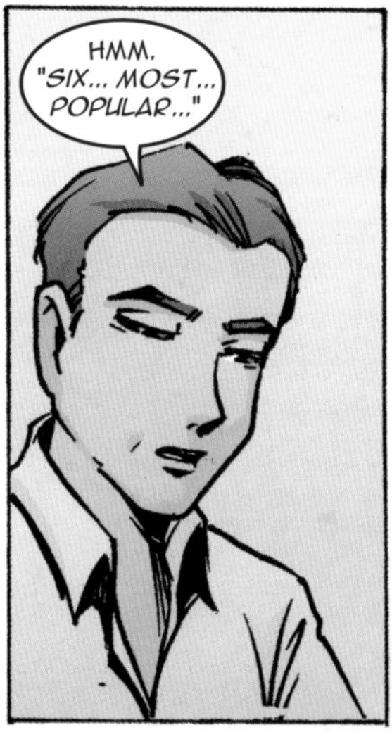
HMM. "SIX... MOST... POPULAR..."
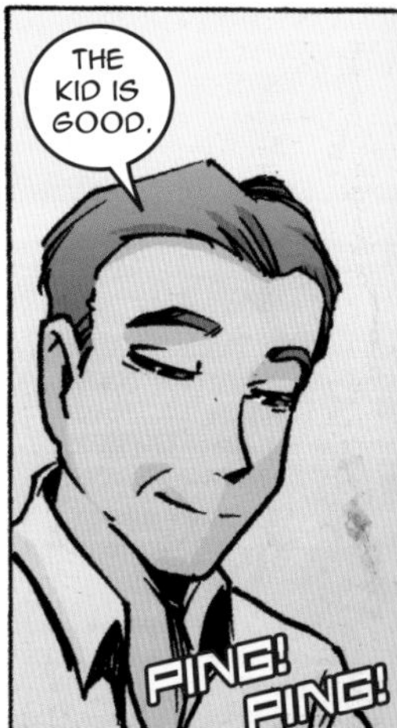
THE KID IS GOOD.
FING! FING!

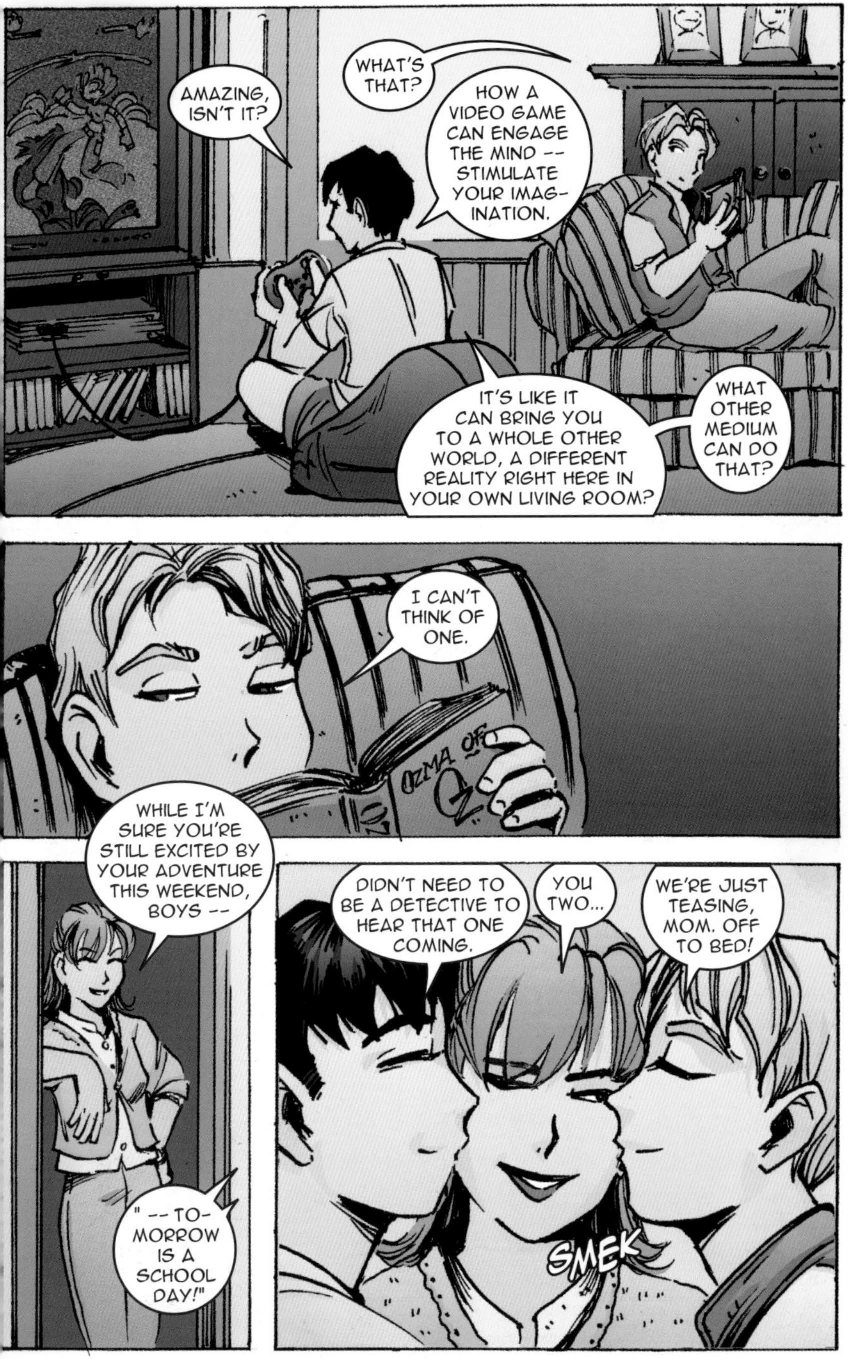
AMAZING, ISN'T IT?
WHAT'S THAT?
HOW A VIDEO GAME CAN ENGAGE THE MIND -- STIMULATE YOUR IMAGINATION.
IT'S LIKE IT CAN BRING YOU TO A WHOLE OTHER WORLD, A DIFFERENT REALITY RIGHT HERE IN YOUR OWN LIVING ROOM?
WHAT OTHER MEDIUM CAN DO THAT?
I CAN'T THINK OF ONE.
WHILE I'M SURE YOU'RE STILL EXCITED BY YOUR ADVENTURE THIS WEEKEND, BOYS --
" -- TOMORROW IS A SCHOOL DAY!"
DIDN'T NEED TO BE A DETECTIVE TO HEAR THAT ONE COMING.
YOU TWO...
WE'RE JUST TEASING, MOM. OFF TO BED!
SMEK

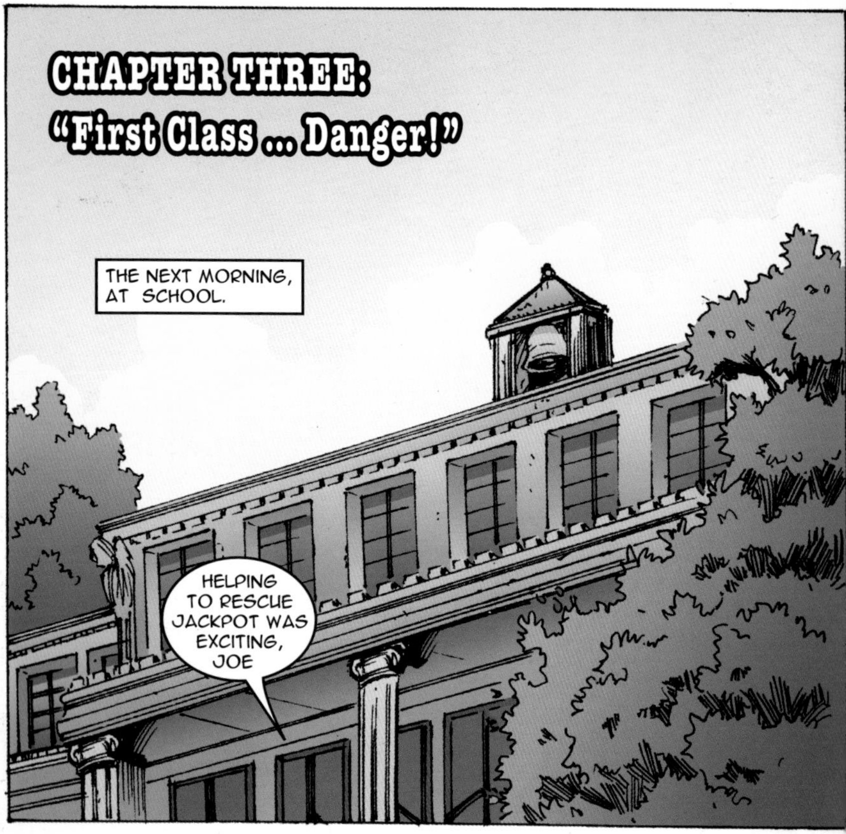
CHAPTER THREE:
"First Class ... Danger!"
THE NEXT MORNING, AT SCHOOL.
HELPING TO RESCUE JACKPOT WAS EXCITING, JOE

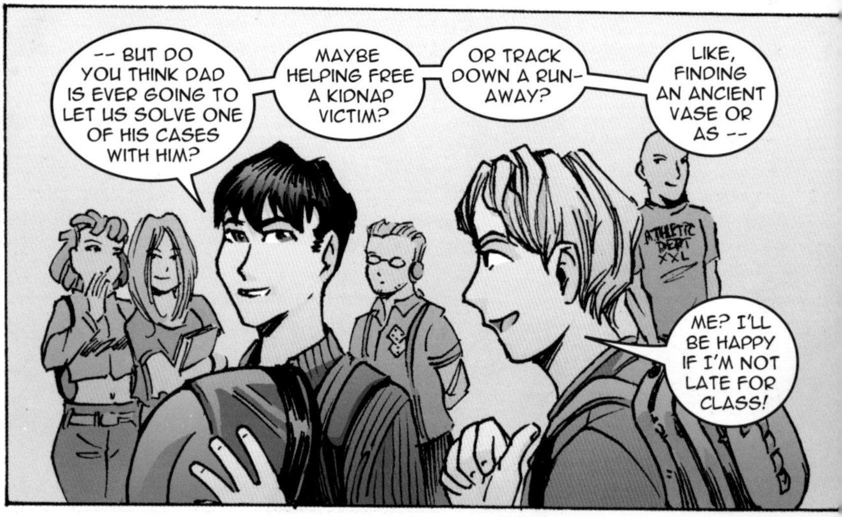
-- BUT DO YOU THINK DAD IS EVER GOING TO LET US SOLVE ONE OF HIS CASES WITH HIM?
MAYBE HELPING FREE A KIDNAP VICTIM?
OR TRACK DOWN A RUN-AWAY?
LIKE, FINDING AN ANCIENT VASE OR AS --
ATHLETIC DEPT XXL
ME? I'LL BE HAPPY IF I'M NOT LATE FOR CLASS!

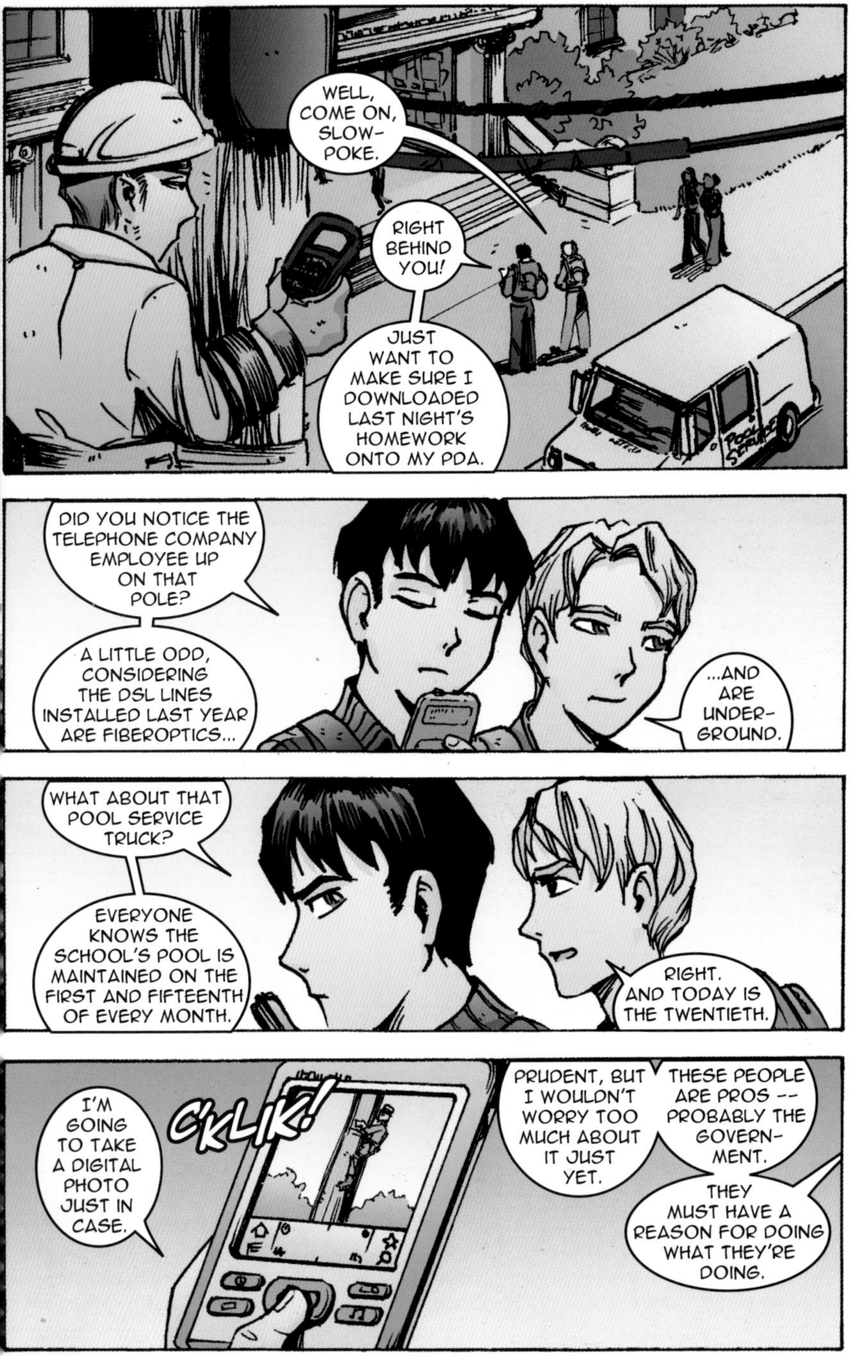

WELL, COME ON, SLOW-POKE.
RIGHT BEHIND YOU!
JUST WANT TO MAKE SURE I DOWNLOADED LAST NIGHT'S HOMEWORK ONTO MY PDA.
DID YOU NOTICE THE TELEPHONE COMPANY EMPLOYEE UP ON THAT POLE?
A LITTLE ODD, CONSIDERING THE DSL LINES INSTALLED LAST YEAR ARE FIBEROPTICS...
...AND ARE UNDER-GROUND.
WHAT ABOUT THAT POOL SERVICE TRUCK?
EVERYONE KNOWS THE SCHOOL'S POOL IS MAINTAINED ON THE FIRST AND FIFTEENTH OF EVERY MONTH.
RIGHT. AND TODAY IS THE TWENTIETH.
I'M GOING TO TAKE A DIGITAL PHOTO JUST IN CASE.
C'KLIK!
PRUDENT, BUT I WOULDN'T WORRY TOO MUCH ABOUT IT JUST YET.
THESE PEOPLE ARE PROS -- PROBABLY THE GOVERN-MENT.
THEY MUST HAVE A REASON FOR DOING WHAT THEY'RE DOING.

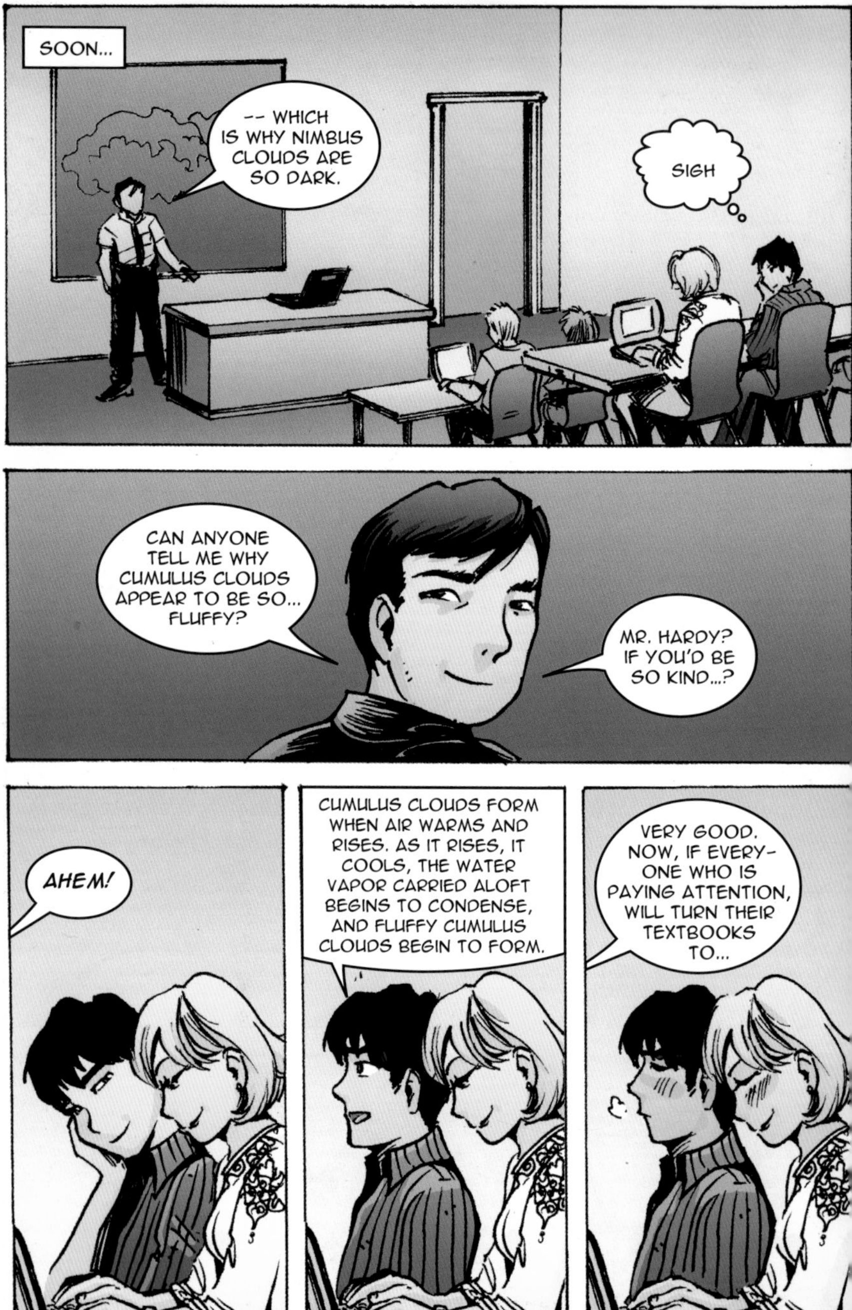
SOON...
-- WHICH IS WHY NIMBUS CLOUDS ARE SO DARK.
SIGH
CAN ANYONE TELL ME WHY CUMULUS CLOUDS APPEAR TO BE SO... FLUFFY?
MR. HARDY? IF YOU'D BE SO KIND...?
AHEM!
CUMULUS CLOUDS FORM WHEN AIR WARMS AND RISES. AS IT RISES, IT COOLS, THE WATER VAPOR CARRIED ALOFT BEGINS TO CONDENSE, AND FLUFFY CUMULUS CLOUDS BEGIN TO FORM.
VERY GOOD. NOW, IF EVERY-ONE WHO IS PAYING ATTENTION, WILL TURN THEIR TEXTBOOKS TO...

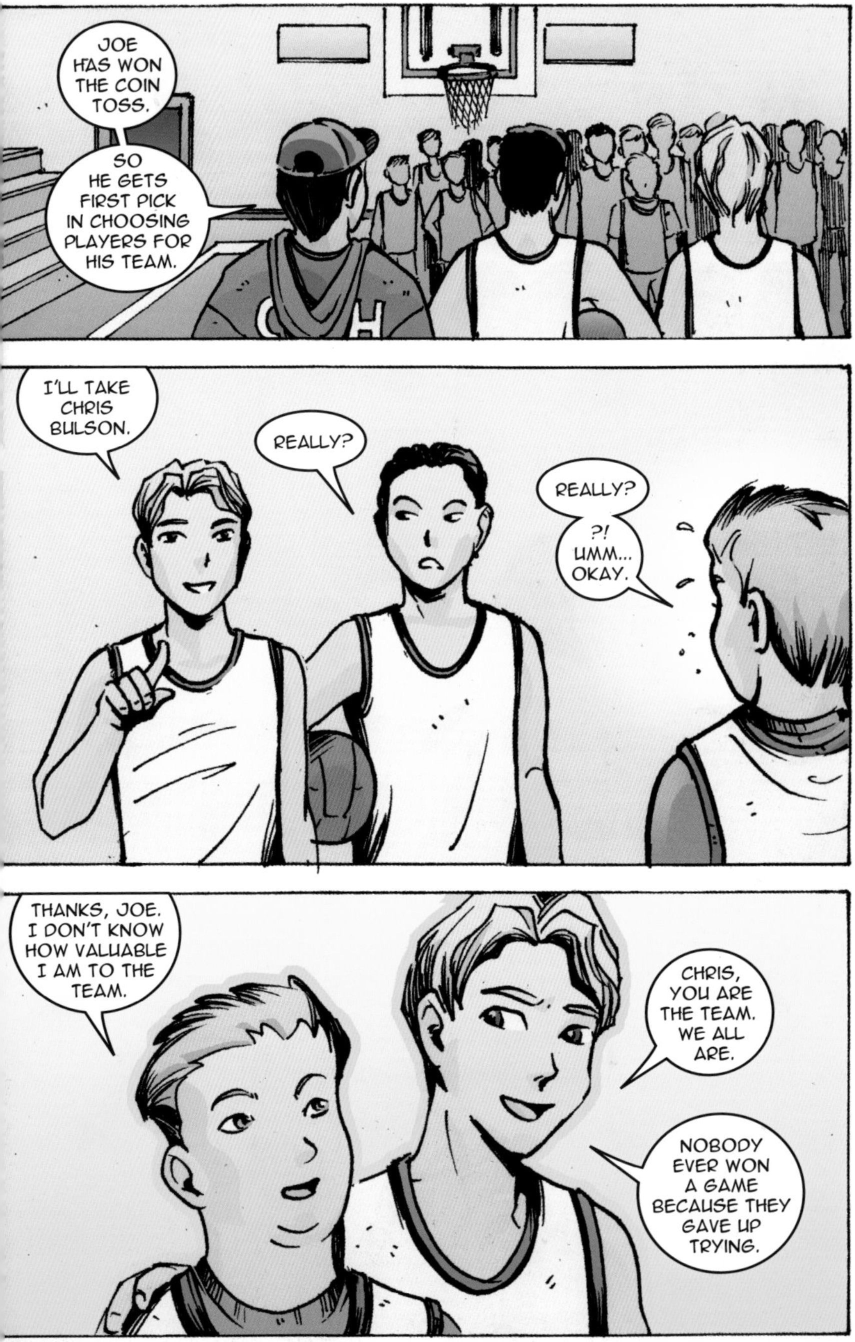
JOE HAS WON THE COIN TOSS.
SO HE GETS FIRST PICK IN CHOOSING PLAYERS FOR HIS TEAM.
I'LL TAKE CHRIS BULSON.
REALLY?
REALLY?
?! UMM... OKAY.
THANKS, JOE. I DON'T KNOW HOW VALUABLE I AM TO THE TEAM.
CHRIS, YOU ARE THE TEAM. WE ALL ARE.
NOBODY EVER WON A GAME BECAUSE THEY GAVE UP TRYING.

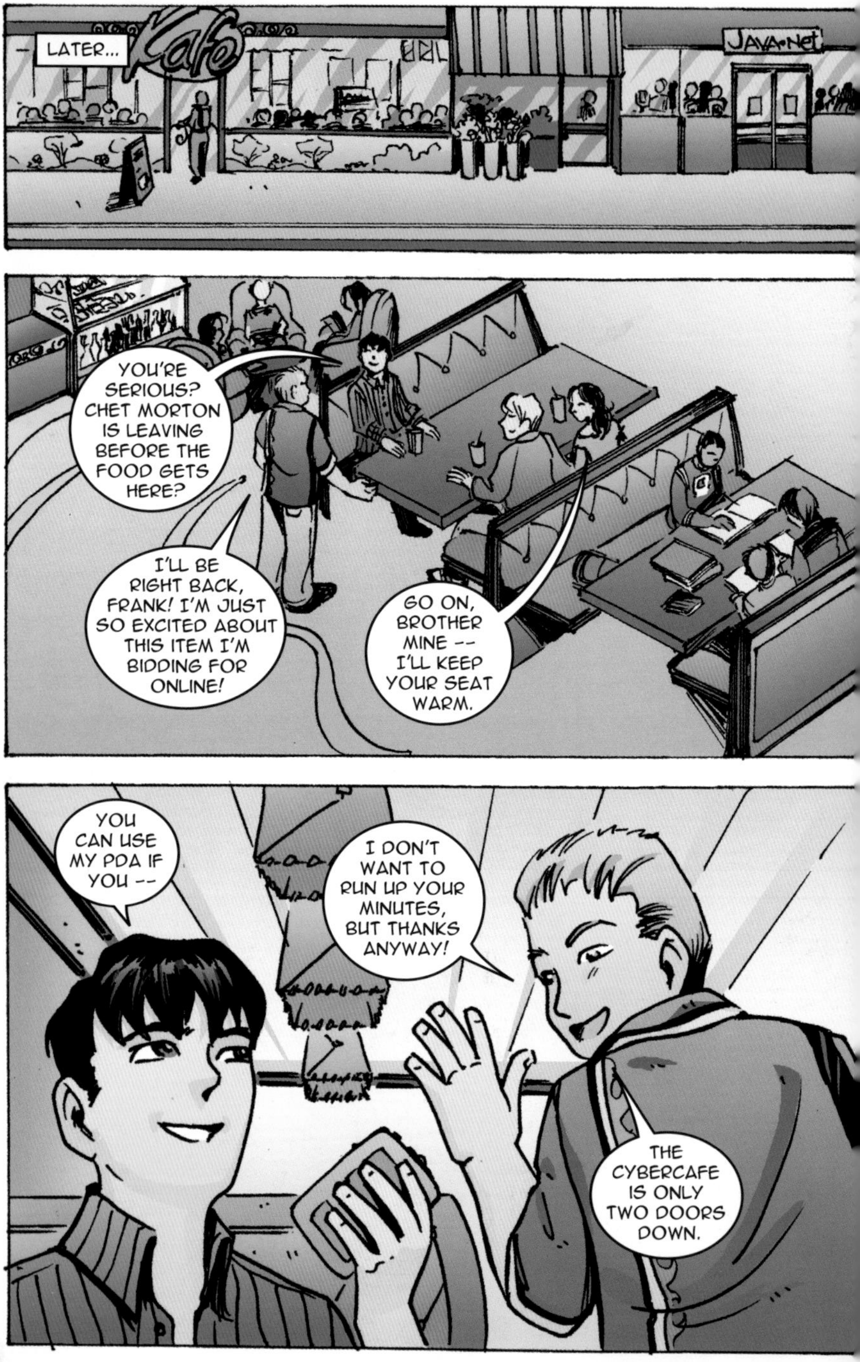
LATER...
Kafe
JAVA•NET
YOU'RE SERIOUS? CHET MORTON IS LEAVING BEFORE THE FOOD GETS HERE?
I'LL BE RIGHT BACK, FRANK! I'M JUST SO EXCITED ABOUT THIS ITEM I'M BIDDING FOR ONLINE!
GO ON, BROTHER MINE -- I'LL KEEP YOUR SEAT WARM.
YOU CAN USE MY PDA IF YOU --
I DON'T WANT TO RUN UP YOUR MINUTES, BUT THANKS ANYWAY!
THE CYBERCAFE IS ONLY TWO DOORS DOWN.

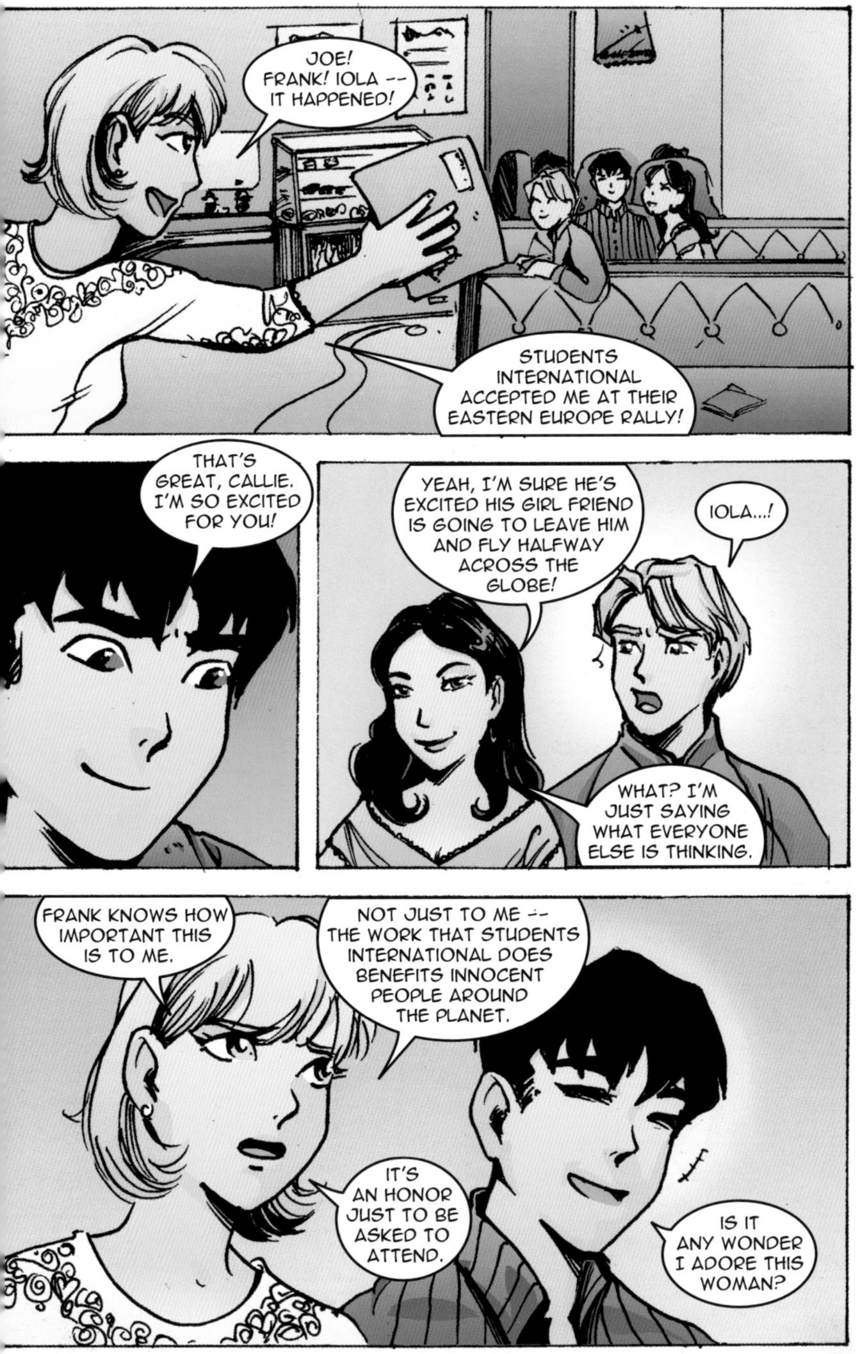
JOE! FRANK! IOLA -- IT HAPPENED!
STUDENTS INTERNATIONAL ACCEPTED ME AT THEIR EASTERN EUROPE RALLY!
THAT'S GREAT, CALLIE. I'M SO EXCITED FOR YOU!
YEAH, I'M SURE HE'S EXCITED HIS GIRL FRIEND IS GOING TO LEAVE HIM AND FLY HALFWAY ACROSS THE GLOBE!
IOLA...!
WHAT? I'M JUST SAYING WHAT EVERYONE ELSE IS THINKING.
FRANK KNOWS HOW IMPORTANT THIS IS TO ME.
NOT JUST TO ME -- THE WORK THAT STUDENTS INTERNATIONAL DOES BENEFITS INNOCENT PEOPLE AROUND THE PLANET.
IT'S AN HONOR JUST TO BE ASKED TO ATTEND.
IS IT ANY WONDER I ADORE THIS WOMAN?

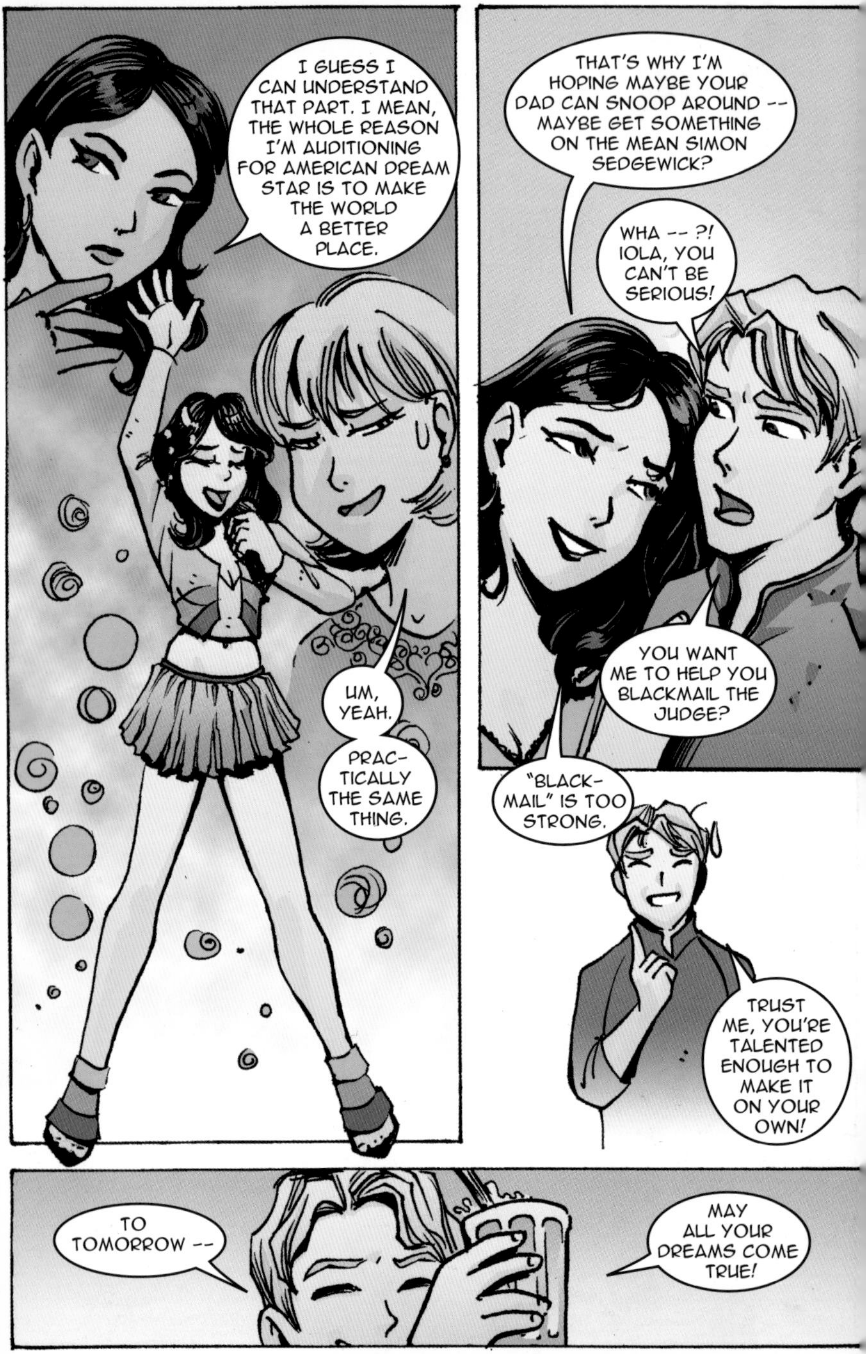
I GUESS I CAN UNDERSTAND THAT PART. I MEAN, THE WHOLE REASON I'M AUDITIONING FOR AMERICAN DREAM STAR IS TO MAKE THE WORLD A BETTER PLACE.
UM, YEAH.
PRAC-TICALLY THE SAME THING.
THAT'S WHY I'M HOPING MAYBE YOUR DAD CAN SNOOP AROUND -- MAYBE GET SOMETHING ON THE MEAN SIMON SEDGEWICK?
WHA -- ?! IOLA, YOU CAN'T BE SERIOUS!
YOU WANT ME TO HELP YOU BLACKMAIL THE JUDGE?
"BLACK-MAIL" IS TOO STRONG.
TRUST ME, YOU'RE TALENTED ENOUGH TO MAKE IT ON YOUR OWN!
TO TOMORROW --
MAY ALL YOUR DREAMS COME TRUE!

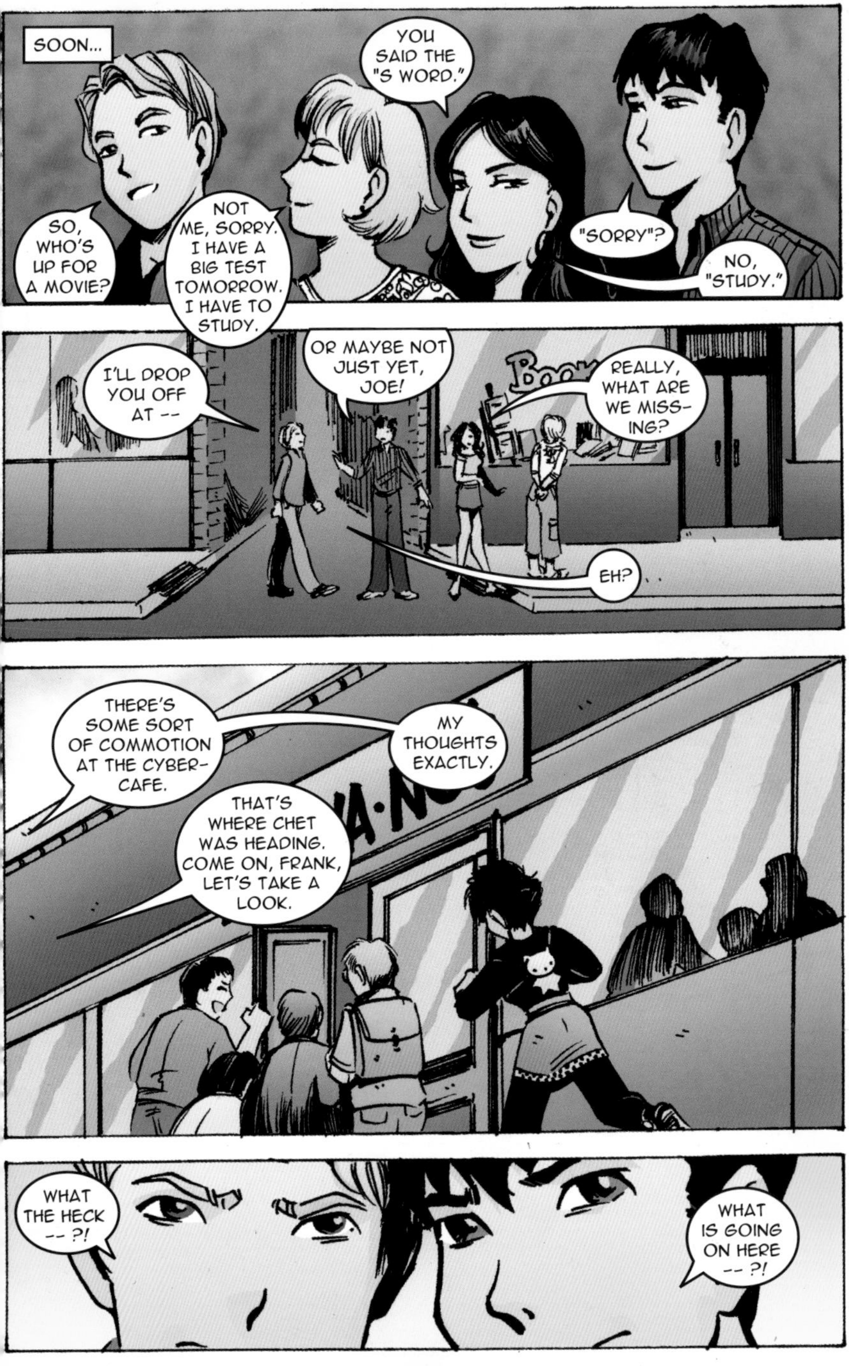
SOON...
SO, WHO'S UP FOR A MOVIE?
NOT ME, SORRY. I HAVE A BIG TEST TOMORROW. I HAVE TO STUDY.
YOU SAID THE "S WORD."
"SORRY"?
NO, "STUDY."
I'LL DROP YOU OFF AT --
OR MAYBE NOT JUST YET, JOE!
REALLY, WHAT ARE WE MISSING?
EH?
THERE'S SOME SORT OF COMMOTION AT THE CYBER-CAFE.
MY THOUGHTS EXACTLY.
THAT'S WHERE CHET WAS HEADING. COME ON, FRANK, LET'S TAKE A LOOK.
WHAT THE HECK -- ?!
WHAT IS GOING ON HERE -- ?!

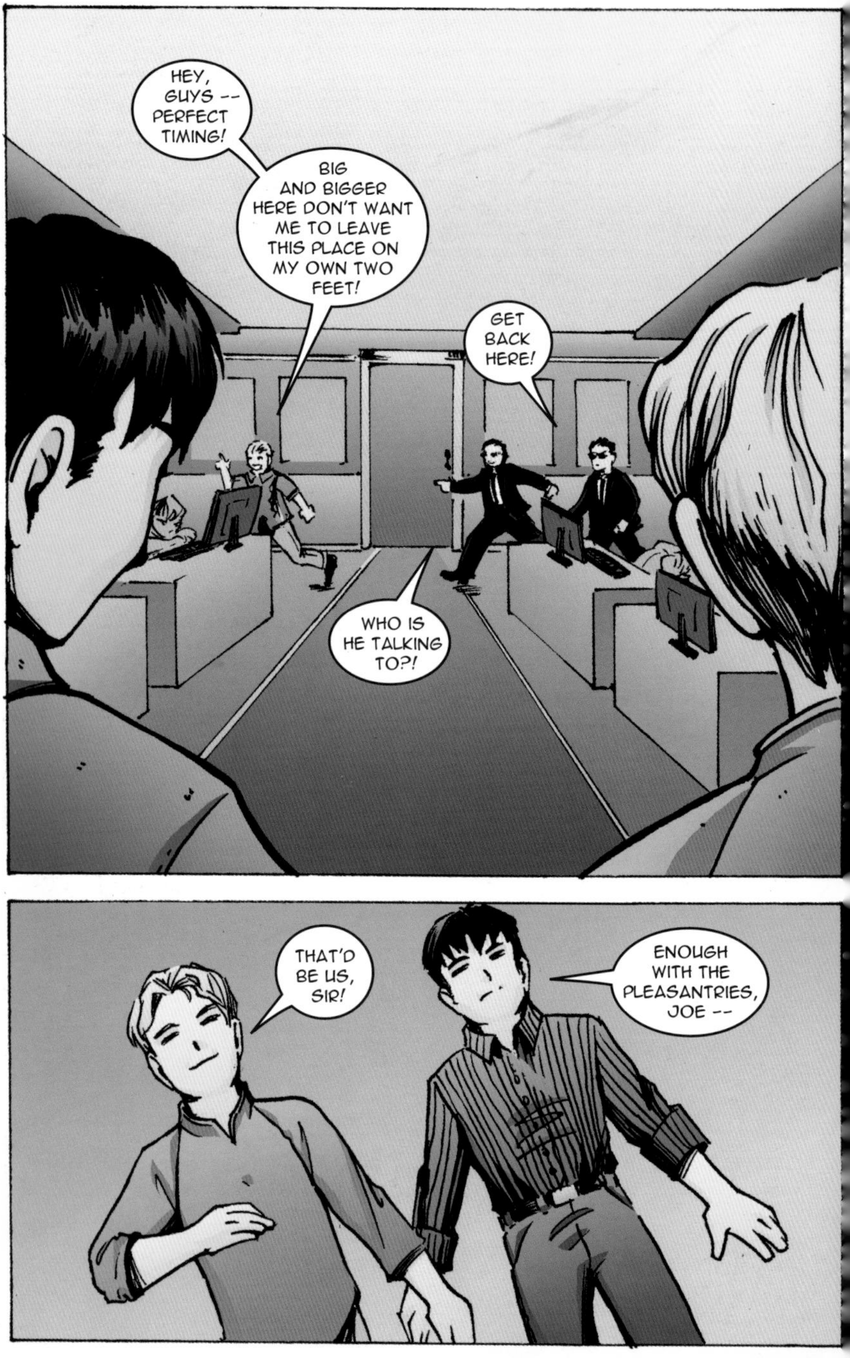
HEY, GUYS -- PERFECT TIMING!
BIG AND BIGGER HERE DON'T WANT ME TO LEAVE THIS PLACE ON MY OWN TWO FEET!
GET BACK HERE!
WHO IS HE TALKING TO?!
THAT'D BE US, SIR!
ENOUGH WITH THE PLEASANTRIES, JOE --

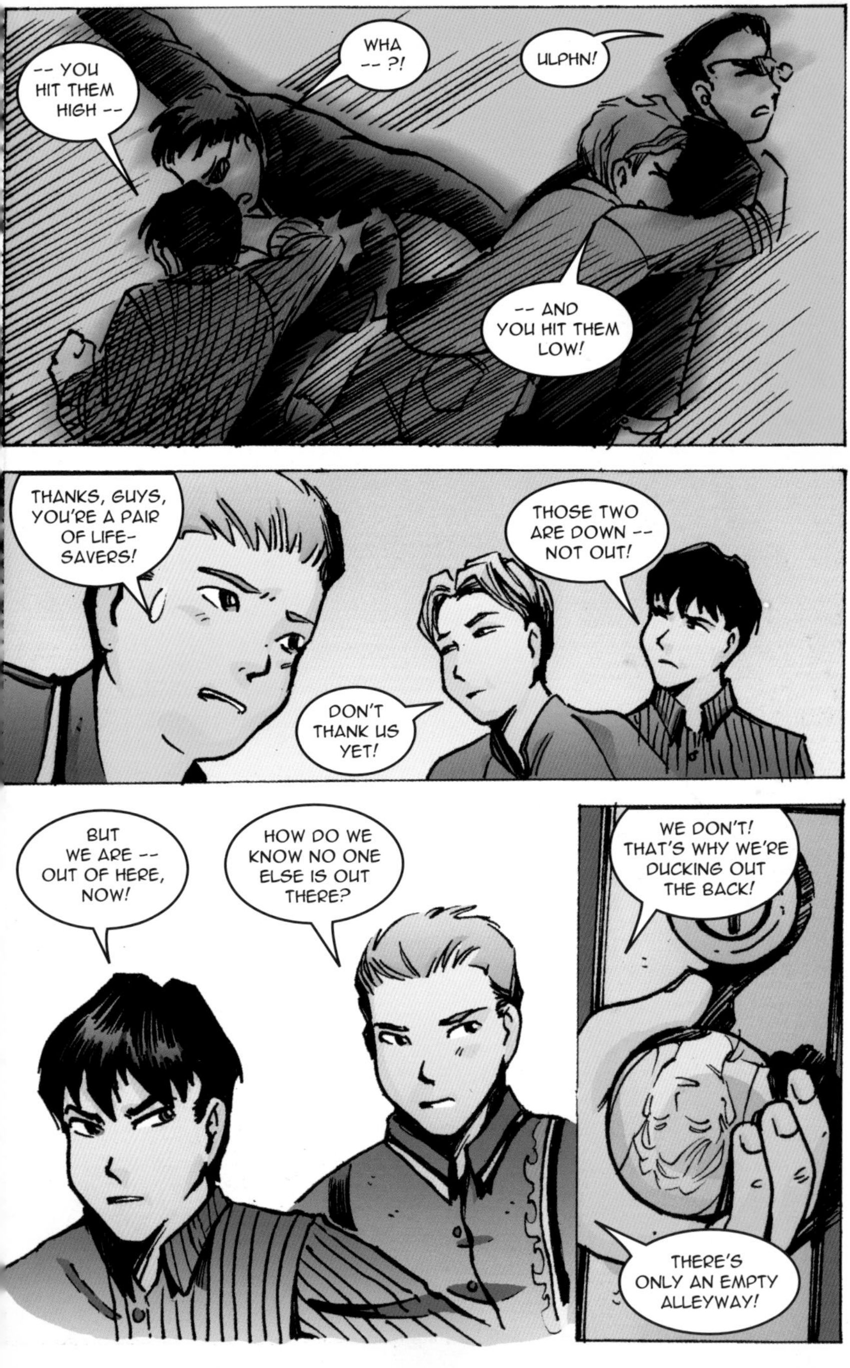
-- YOU HIT THEM HIGH --
WHA -- ?!
ULPHN!
-- AND YOU HIT THEM LOW!
THANKS, GUYS, YOU'RE A PAIR OF LIFE-SAVERS!
THOSE TWO ARE DOWN -- NOT OUT!
DON'T THANK US YET!
BUT WE ARE -- OUT OF HERE, NOW!
HOW DO WE KNOW NO ONE ELSE IS OUT THERE?
WE DON'T! THAT'S WHY WE'RE DUCKING OUT THE BACK!
THERE'S ONLY AN EMPTY ALLEYWAY!

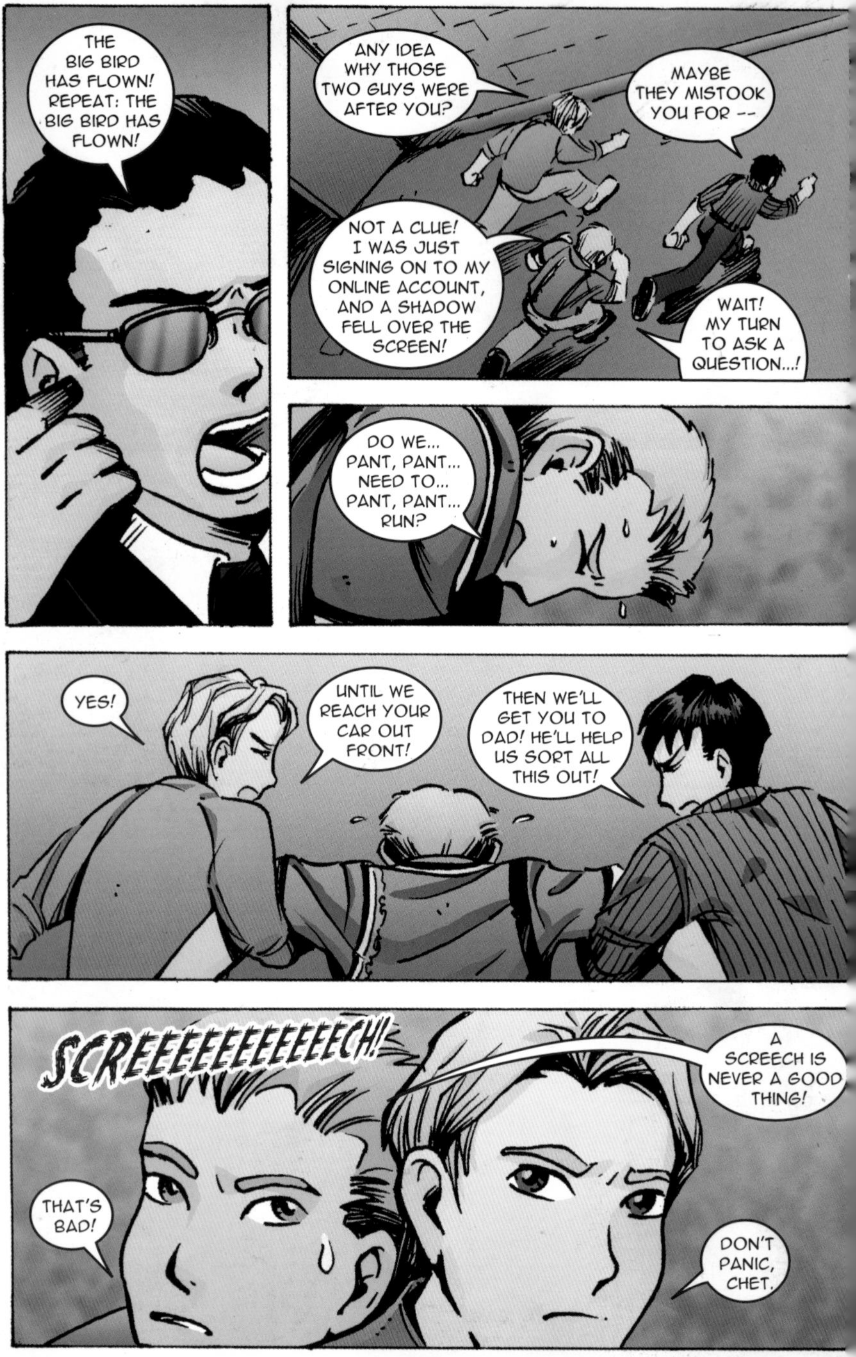
THE BIG BIRD HAS FLOWN! REPEAT: THE BIG BIRD HAS FLOWN!
ANY IDEA WHY THOSE TWO GUYS WERE AFTER YOU?
MAYBE THEY MISTOOK YOU FOR --
NOT A CLUE! I WAS JUST SIGNING ON TO MY ONLINE ACCOUNT, AND A SHADOW FELL OVER THE SCREEN!
WAIT! MY TURN TO ASK A QUESTION...!
DO WE... PANT, PANT... NEED TO... PANT, PANT... RUN?
YES!
UNTIL WE REACH YOUR CAR OUT FRONT!
THEN WE'LL GET YOU TO DAD! HE'LL HELP US SORT ALL THIS OUT!
SCREEEEEEEEEEEECH!
A SCREECH IS NEVER A GOOD THING!
THAT'S BAD!
DON'T PANIC, CHET.

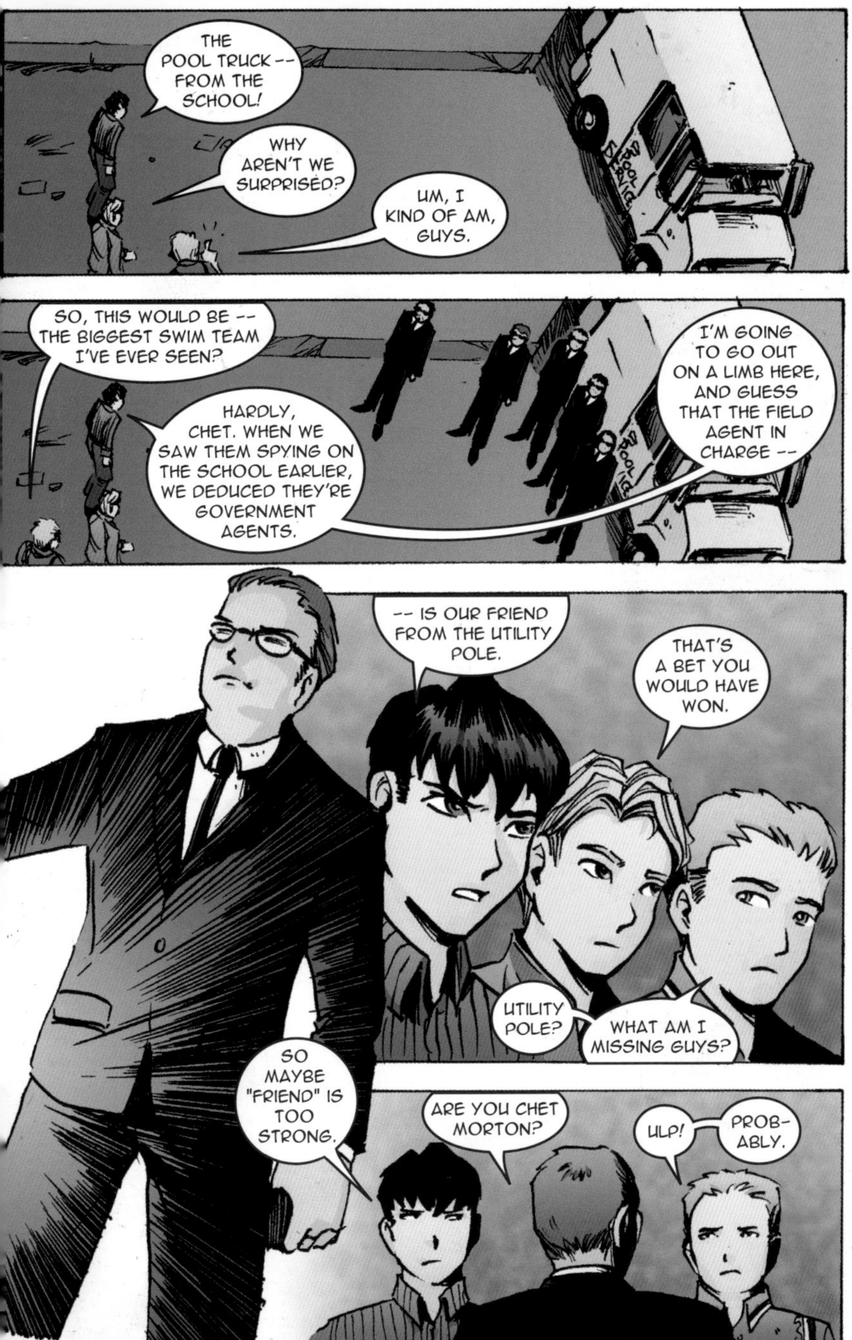

THE POOL TRUCK -- FROM THE SCHOOL!
WHY AREN'T WE SURPRISED?
UM, I KIND OF AM, GUYS.
POOL SERVICE
SO, THIS WOULD BE -- THE BIGGEST SWIM TEAM I'VE EVER SEEN?
HARDLY, CHET. WHEN WE SAW THEM SPYING ON THE SCHOOL EARLIER, WE DEDUCED THEY'RE GOVERNMENT AGENTS.
I'M GOING TO GO OUT ON A LIMB HERE, AND GUESS THAT THE FIELD AGENT IN CHARGE --
-- IS OUR FRIEND FROM THE UTILITY POLE.
THAT'S A BET YOU WOULD HAVE WON.
UTILITY POLE?
WHAT AM I MISSING GUYS?
SO MAYBE "FRIEND" IS TOO STRONG.
ARE YOU CHET MORTON?
ULP!
PROB-ABLY.

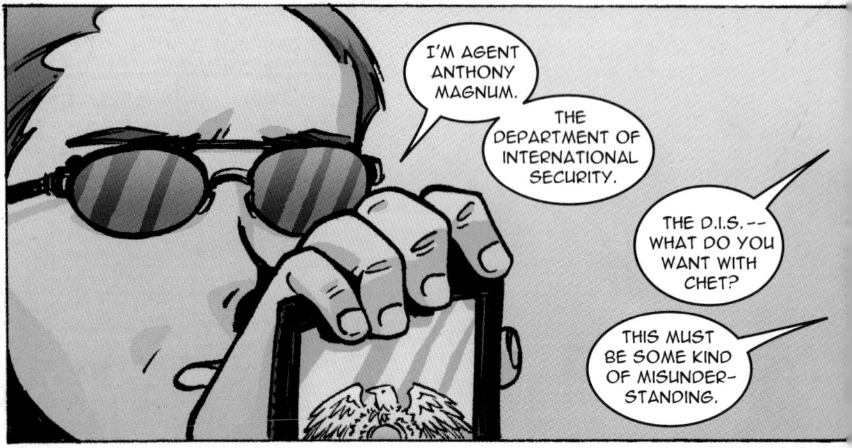
I'M AGENT ANTHONY MAGNUM.
THE DEPARTMENT OF INTERNATIONAL SECURITY.
THE D.I.S.-- WHAT DO YOU WANT WITH CHET?
THIS MUST BE SOME KIND OF MISUNDER-STANDING.

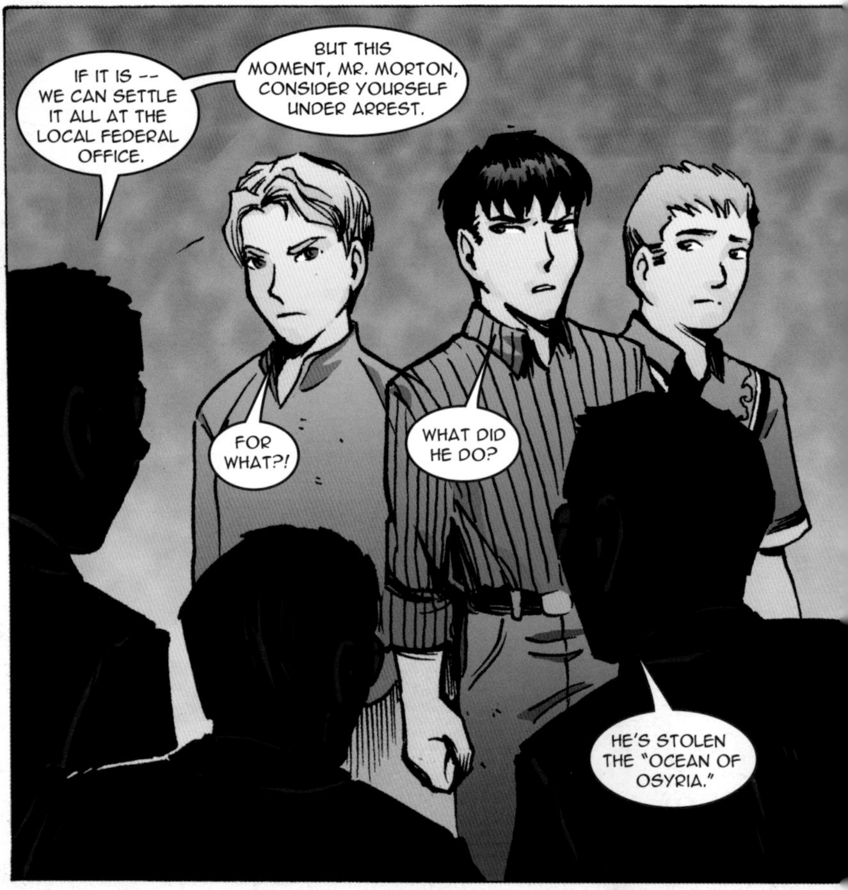
IF IT IS -- WE CAN SETTLE IT ALL AT THE LOCAL FEDERAL OFFICE.
BUT THIS MOMENT, MR. MORTON, CONSIDER YOURSELF UNDER ARREST.
FOR WHAT?!
WHAT DID HE DO?
HE'S STOLEN THE "OCEAN OF OSYRIA."

CHAPTER FOUR:
"Jailhouse Rock...?!"

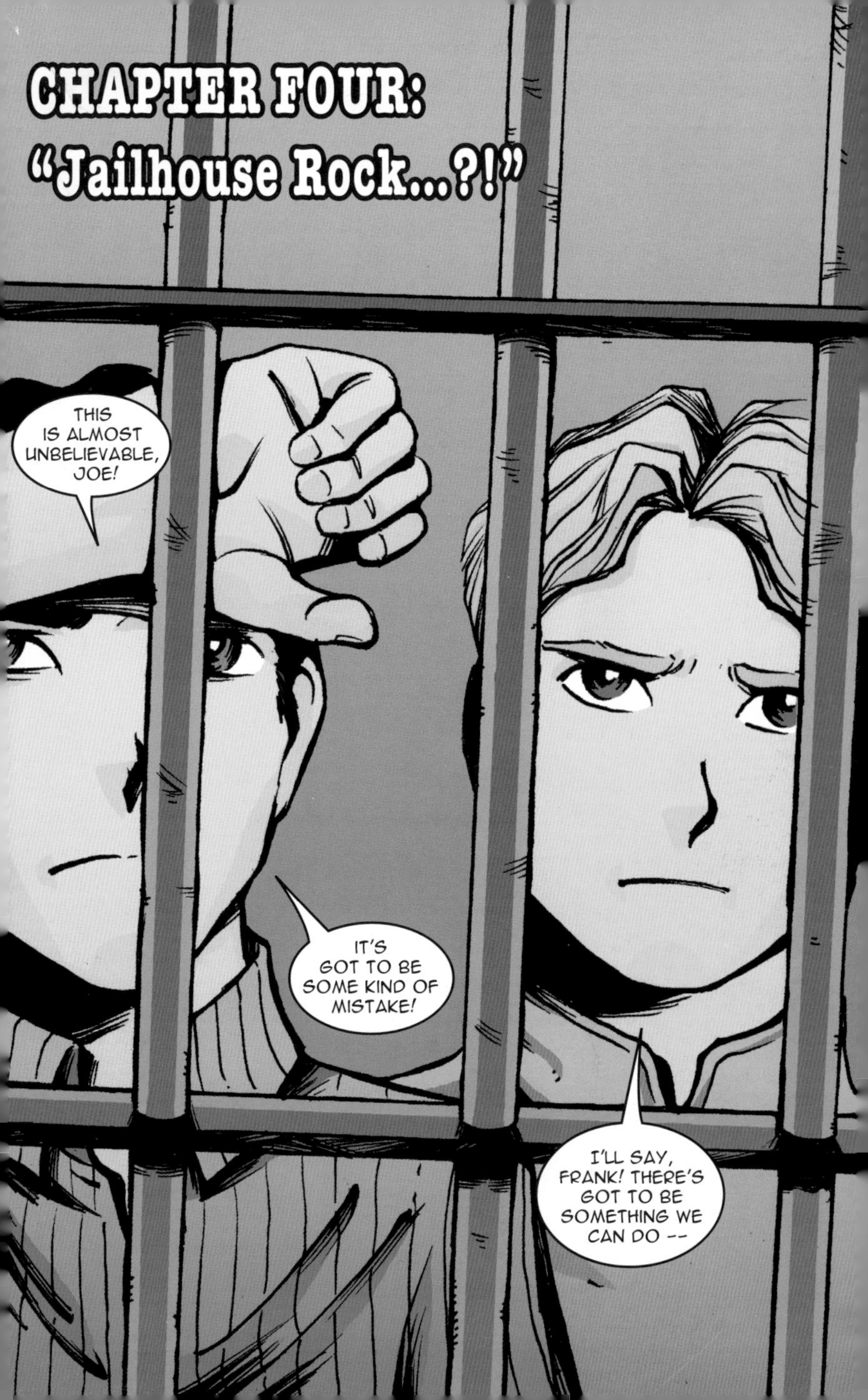
THIS IS ALMOST UNBELIEVABLE, JOE!
IT'S GOT TO BE SOME KIND OF MISTAKE!
I'LL SAY, FRANK! THERE'S GOT TO BE SOMETHING WE CAN DO --

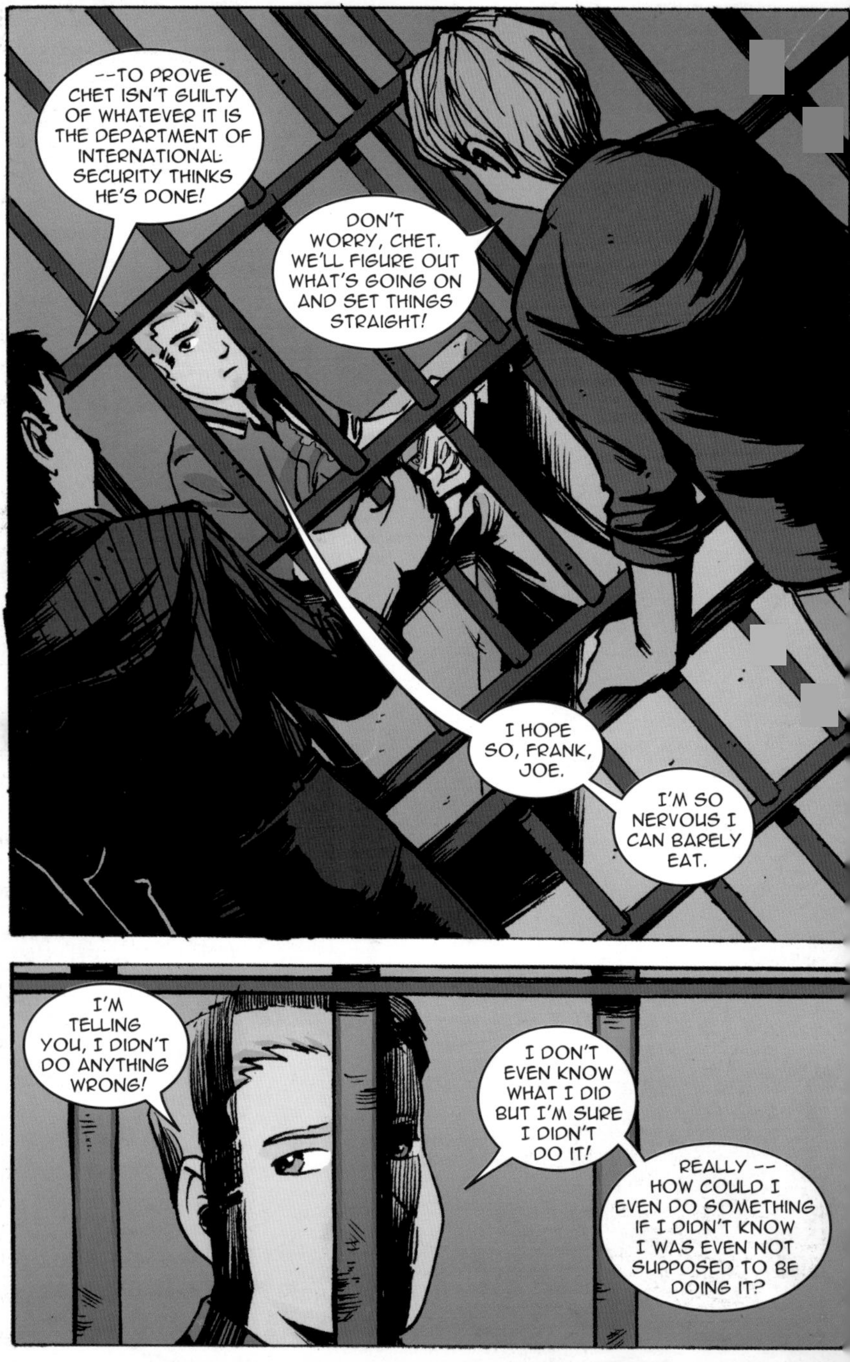
--TO PROVE CHET ISN'T GUILTY OF WHATEVER IT IS THE DEPARTMENT OF INTERNATIONAL SECURITY THINKS HE'S DONE!
DON'T WORRY, CHET. WE'LL FIGURE OUT WHAT'S GOING ON AND SET THINGS STRAIGHT!
I HOPE SO, FRANK, JOE.
I'M SO NERVOUS I CAN BARELY EAT.
I'M TELLING YOU, I DIDN'T DO ANYTHING WRONG!
I DON'T EVEN KNOW WHAT I DID BUT I'M SURE I DIDN'T DO IT!
REALLY -- HOW COULD I EVEN DO SOMETHING IF I DIDN'T KNOW I WAS EVEN NOT SUPPOSED TO BE DOING IT?

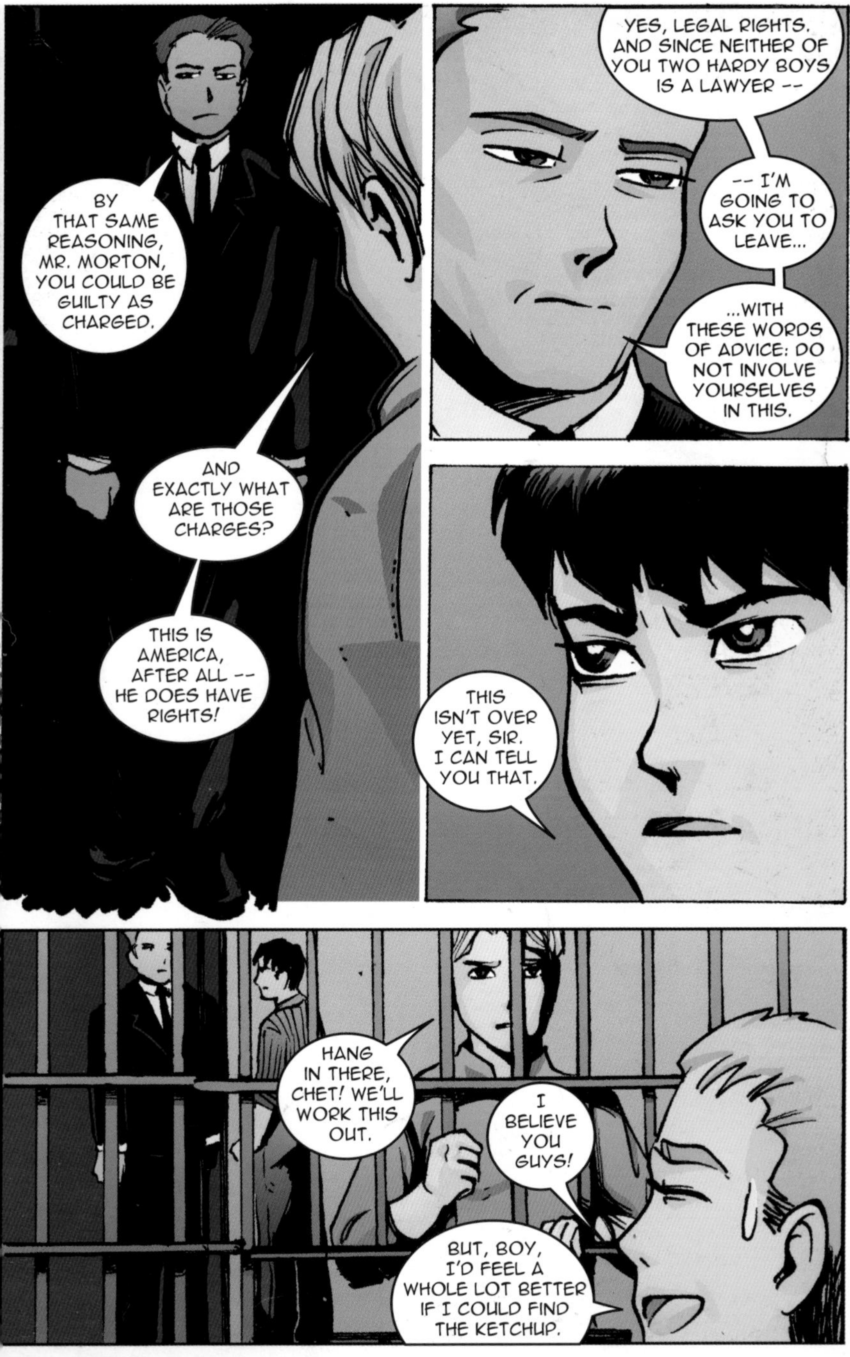
BY THAT SAME REASONING, MR. MORTON, YOU COULD BE GUILTY AS CHARGED.
AND EXACTLY WHAT ARE THOSE CHARGES?
THIS IS AMERICA, AFTER ALL -- HE DOES HAVE RIGHTS!
YES, LEGAL RIGHTS. AND SINCE NEITHER OF YOU TWO HARDY BOYS IS A LAWYER --
-- I'M GOING TO ASK YOU TO LEAVE...
...WITH THESE WORDS OF ADVICE: DO NOT INVOLVE YOURSELVES IN THIS.
THIS ISN'T OVER YET, SIR. I CAN TELL YOU THAT.
HANG IN THERE, CHET! WE'LL WORK THIS OUT.
I BELIEVE YOU GUYS!
BUT, BOY, I'D FEEL A WHOLE LOT BETTER IF I COULD FIND THE KETCHUP.

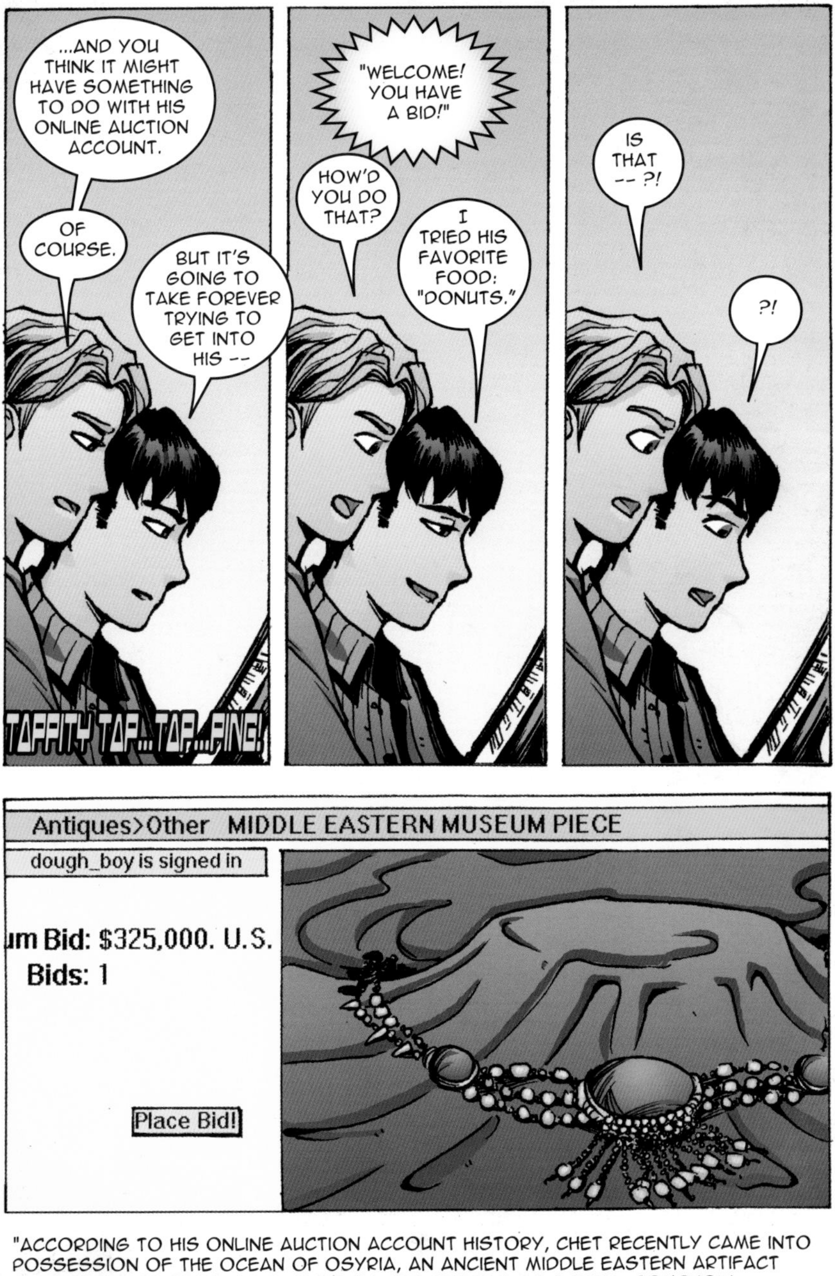
...AND YOU THINK IT MIGHT HAVE SOMETHING TO DO WITH HIS ONLINE AUCTION ACCOUNT.
OF COURSE.
BUT IT'S GOING TO TAKE FOREVER TRYING TO GET INTO HIS --
TAPPITY TAP...TAP...PING!
"WELCOME! YOU HAVE A BID!"
HOW'D YOU DO THAT?
I TRIED HIS FAVORITE FOOD: "DONUTS."
IS THAT -- ?!
?!
Antiques>Other MIDDLE EASTERN MUSEUM PIECE
dough_boy is signed in
um Bid: $325,000. U.S.
Bids: 1
Place Bid!

"ACCORDING TO HIS ONLINE AUCTION ACCOUNT HISTORY, CHET RECENTLY CAME INTO POSSESSION OF THE OCEAN OF OSYRIA, AN ANCIENT MIDDLE EASTERN ARTIFACT THAT WAS LAST SEEN IN THE NATIONAL ART MUSEUM OF OSYRIA. SOMEHOW -- SOME WAY -- THIS SEVERAL CENTURY OLD NECKLACE WAS STOLEN AND MADE ITS WAY TO THE OTHERWISE HAPLESS CHET MORTON!"

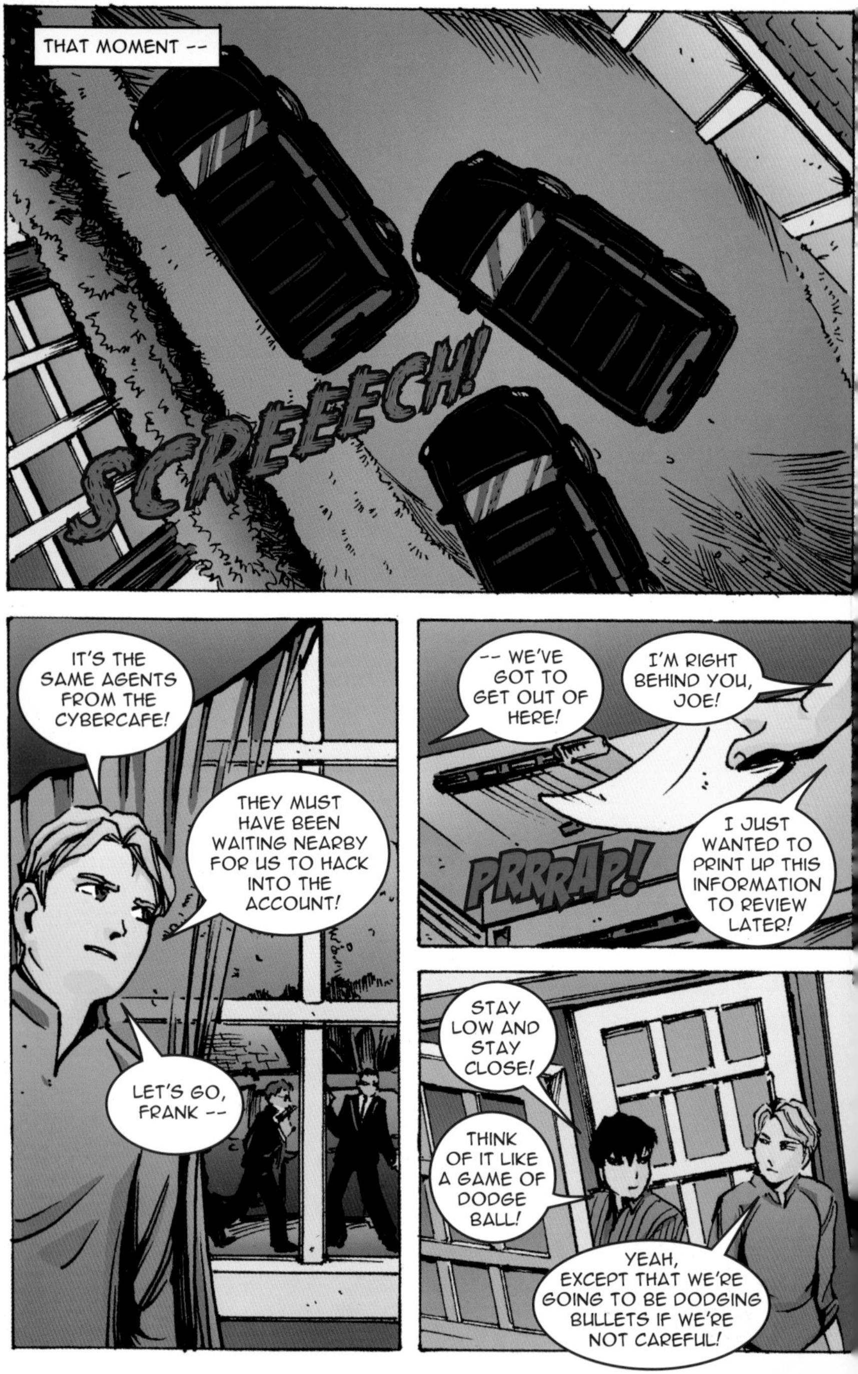
THAT MOMENT --
SCREEECH!
IT'S THE SAME AGENTS FROM THE CYBERCAFE!
THEY MUST HAVE BEEN WAITING NEARBY FOR US TO HACK INTO THE ACCOUNT!
LET'S GO, FRANK --
-- WE'VE GOT TO GET OUT OF HERE!
I'M RIGHT BEHIND YOU, JOE!
PRRRAP!
I JUST WANTED TO PRINT UP THIS INFORMATION TO REVIEW LATER!
STAY LOW AND STAY CLOSE!
THINK OF IT LIKE A GAME OF DODGE BALL!
YEAH, EXCEPT THAT WE'RE GOING TO BE DODGING BULLETS IF WE'RE NOT CAREFUL!

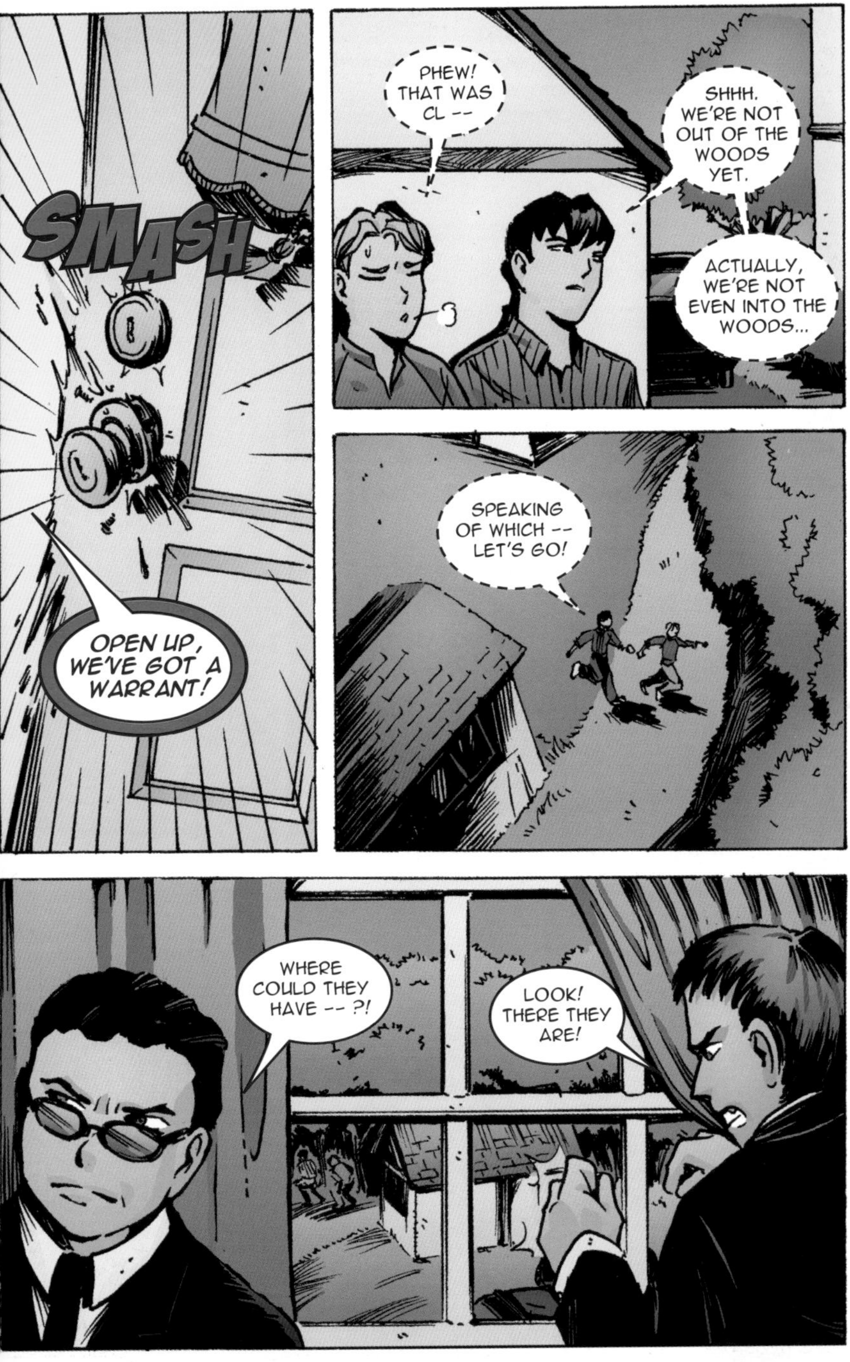
SMASH
OPEN UP, WE'VE GOT A WARRANT!
PHEW! THAT WAS CL --
SHHH. WE'RE NOT OUT OF THE WOODS YET.
ACTUALLY, WE'RE NOT EVEN INTO THE WOODS...
SPEAKING OF WHICH -- LET'S GO!
WHERE COULD THEY HAVE -- ?!
LOOK! THERE THEY ARE!

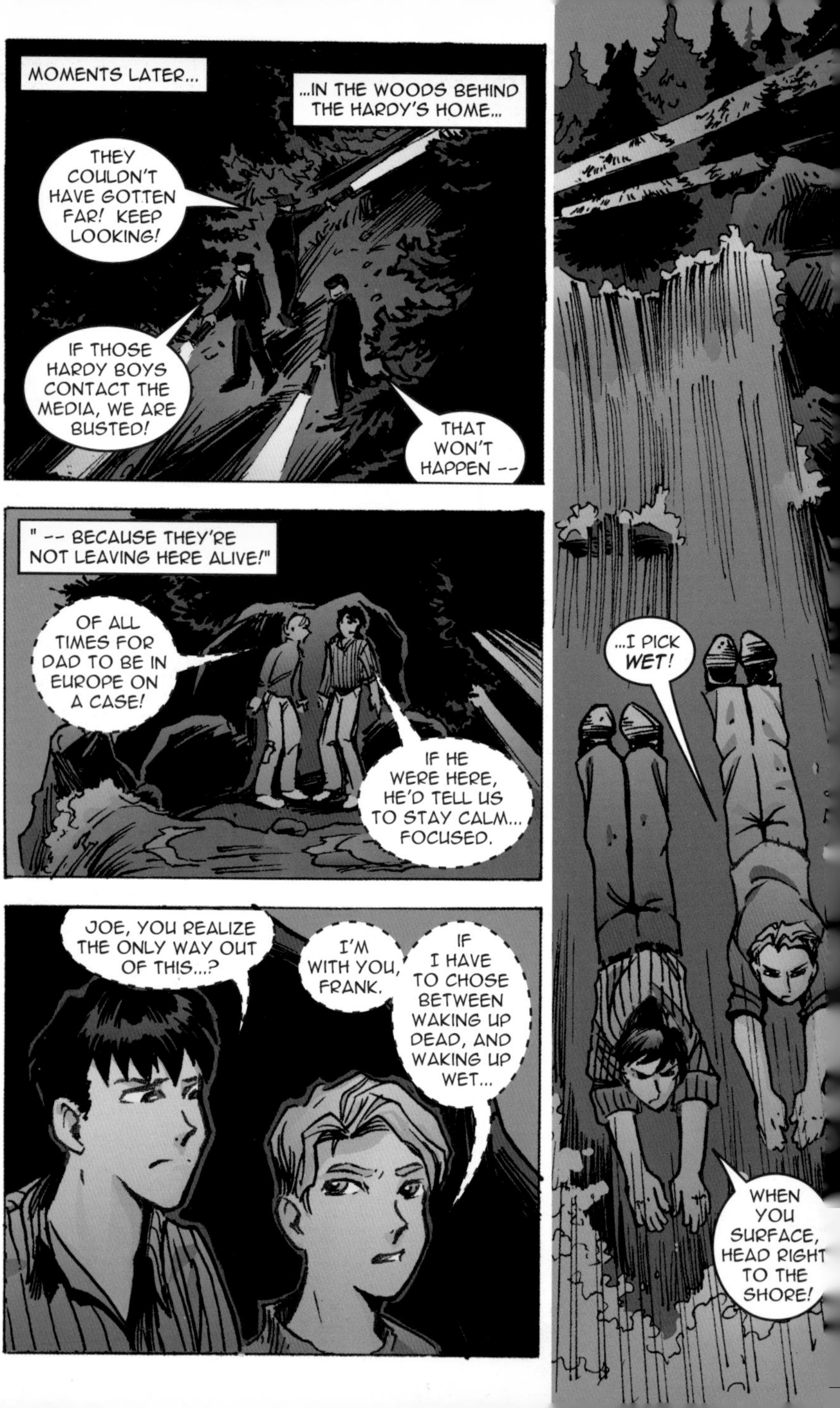
MOMENTS LATER...
...IN THE WOODS BEHIND THE HARDY'S HOME...
THEY COULDN'T HAVE GOTTEN FAR! KEEP LOOKING!
IF THOSE HARDY BOYS CONTACT THE MEDIA, WE ARE BUSTED!
THAT WON'T HAPPEN --
" -- BECAUSE THEY'RE NOT LEAVING HERE ALIVE!"
OF ALL TIMES FOR DAD TO BE IN EUROPE ON A CASE!
IF HE WERE HERE, HE'D TELL US TO STAY CALM... FOCUSED.
JOE, YOU REALIZE THE ONLY WAY OUT OF THIS...?
I'M WITH YOU, FRANK.
IF I HAVE TO CHOSE BETWEEN WAKING UP DEAD, AND WAKING UP WET...
...I PICK *WET*!
WHEN YOU SURFACE, HEAD RIGHT TO THE SHORE!

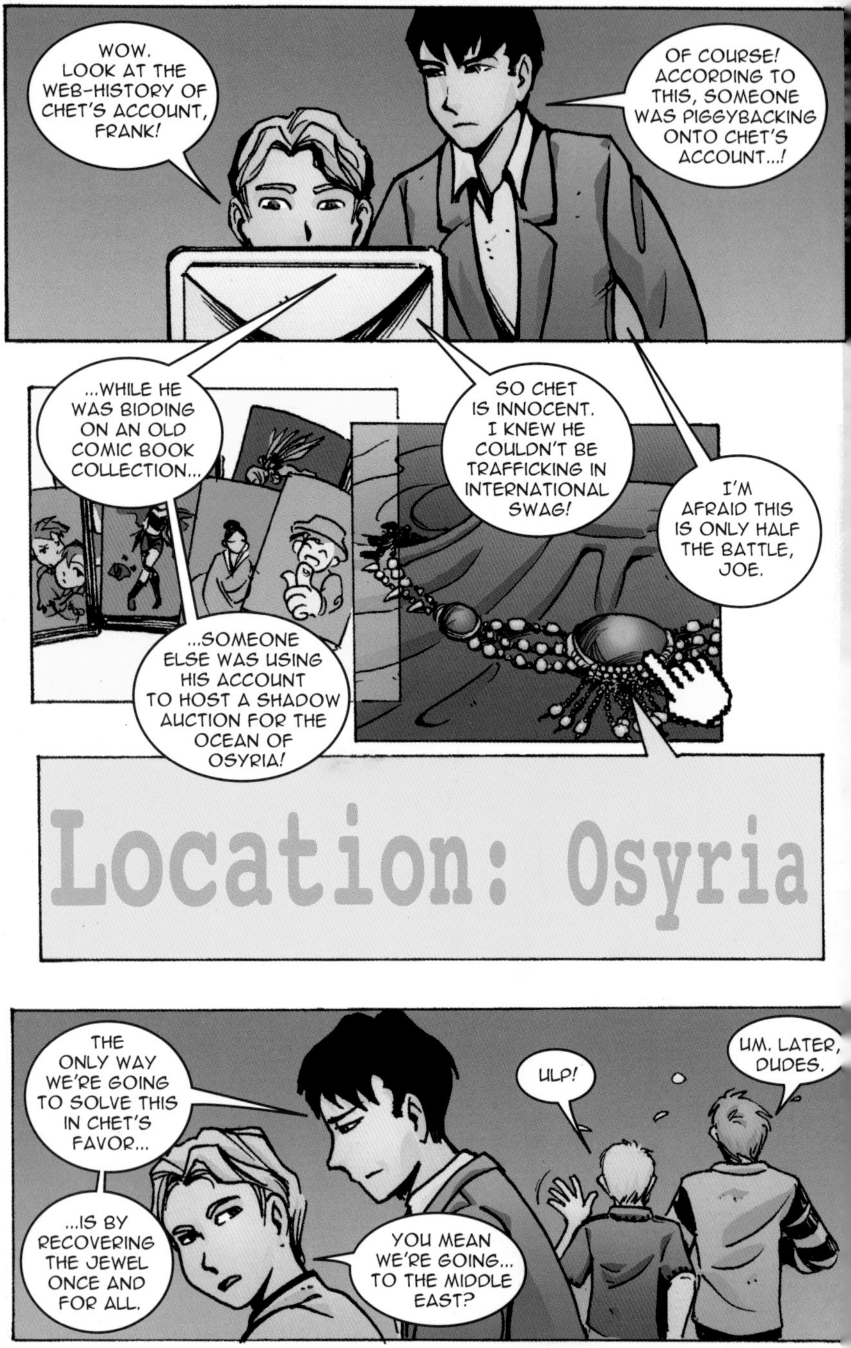
WOW. LOOK AT THE WEB-HISTORY OF CHET'S ACCOUNT, FRANK!
OF COURSE! ACCORDING TO THIS, SOMEONE WAS PIGGYBACKING ONTO CHET'S ACCOUNT...!
...WHILE HE WAS BIDDING ON AN OLD COMIC BOOK COLLECTION...
...SOMEONE ELSE WAS USING HIS ACCOUNT TO HOST A SHADOW AUCTION FOR THE OCEAN OF OSYRIA!
SO CHET IS INNOCENT. I KNEW HE COULDN'T BE TRAFFICKING IN INTERNATIONAL SWAG!
I'M AFRAID THIS IS ONLY HALF THE BATTLE, JOE.
Location: Osyria
THE ONLY WAY WE'RE GOING TO SOLVE THIS IN CHET'S FAVOR...
...IS BY RECOVERING THE JEWEL ONCE AND FOR ALL.
YOU MEAN WE'RE GOING... TO THE MIDDLE EAST?
ULP!
UM. LATER, DUDES.

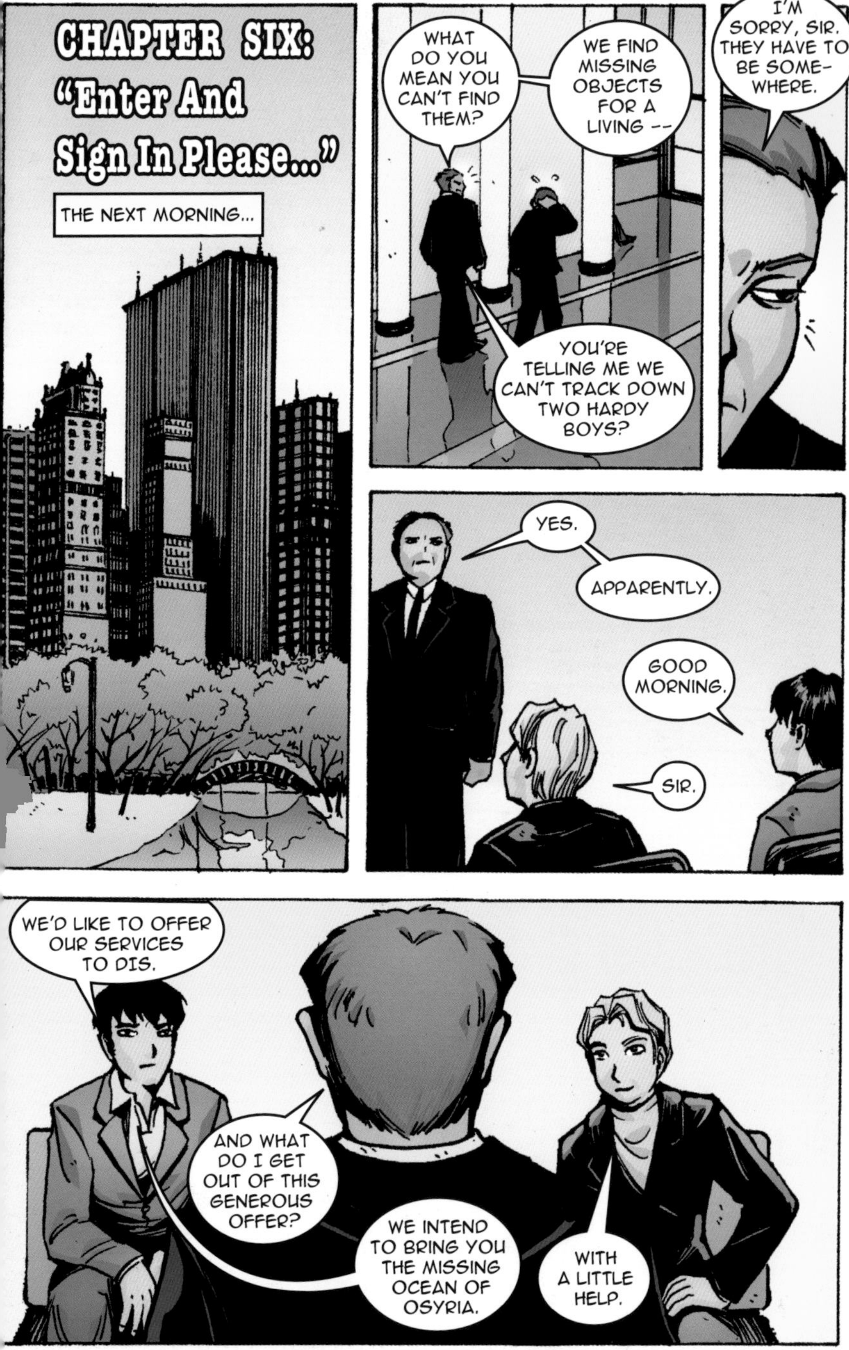
CHAPTER SIX:
"Enter And Sign In Please..."
THE NEXT MORNING...
WHAT DO YOU MEAN YOU CAN'T FIND THEM?
WE FIND MISSING OBJECTS FOR A LIVING --
YOU'RE TELLING ME WE CAN'T TRACK DOWN TWO HARDY BOYS?
I'M SORRY, SIR. THEY HAVE TO BE SOME-WHERE.
YES.
APPARENTLY.
GOOD MORNING.
SIR.
WE'D LIKE TO OFFER OUR SERVICES TO DIS.
AND WHAT DO I GET OUT OF THIS GENEROUS OFFER?
WE INTEND TO BRING YOU THE MISSING OCEAN OF OSYRIA.
WITH A LITTLE HELP.

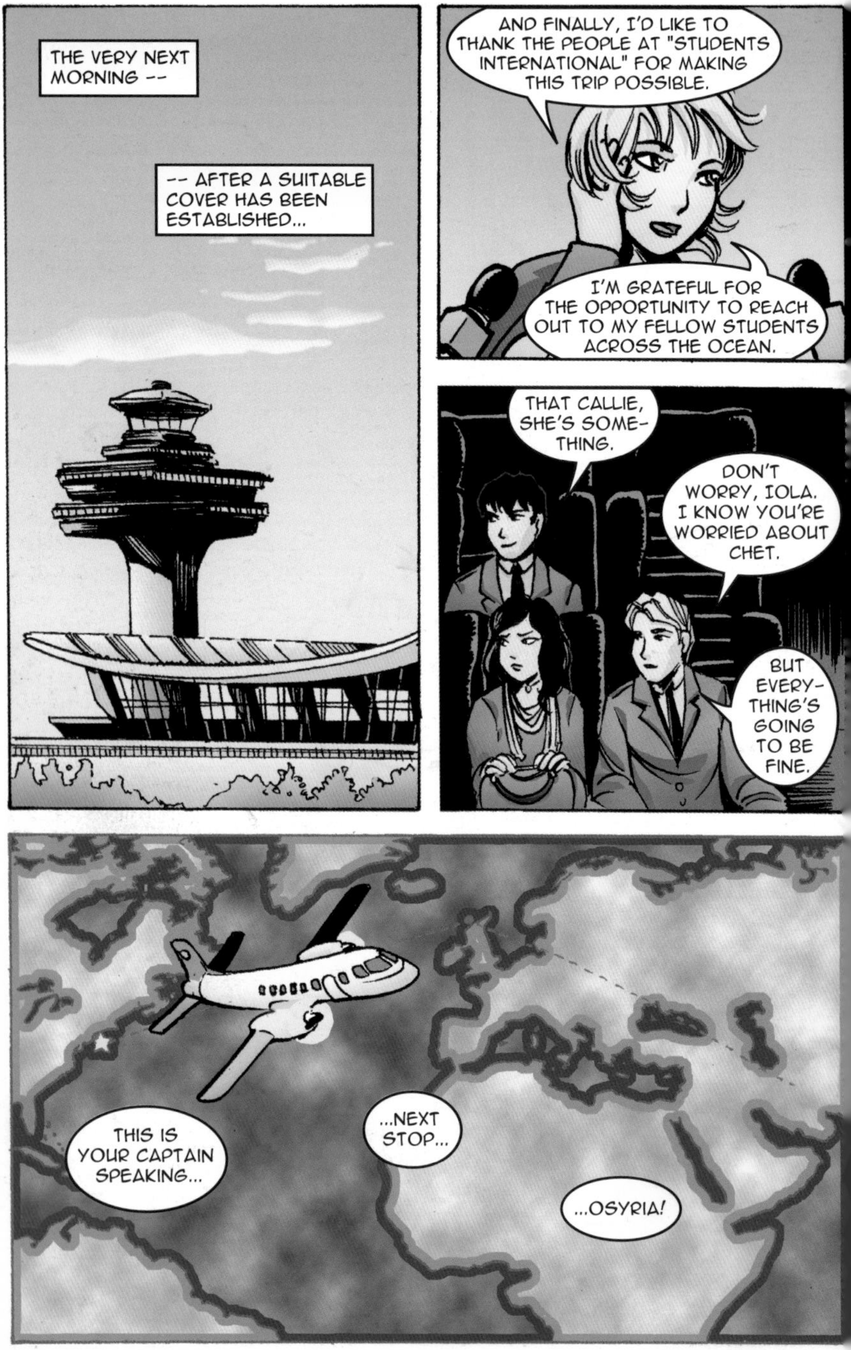
THE VERY NEXT MORNING --
-- AFTER A SUITABLE COVER HAS BEEN ESTABLISHED...
AND FINALLY, I'D LIKE TO THANK THE PEOPLE AT "STUDENTS INTERNATIONAL" FOR MAKING THIS TRIP POSSIBLE.
I'M GRATEFUL FOR THE OPPORTUNITY TO REACH OUT TO MY FELLOW STUDENTS ACROSS THE OCEAN.
THAT CALLIE, SHE'S SOME-THING.
DON'T WORRY, IOLA. I KNOW YOU'RE WORRIED ABOUT CHET.
BUT EVERY-THING'S GOING TO BE FINE.
THIS IS YOUR CAPTAIN SPEAKING...
...NEXT STOP...
...OSYRIA!

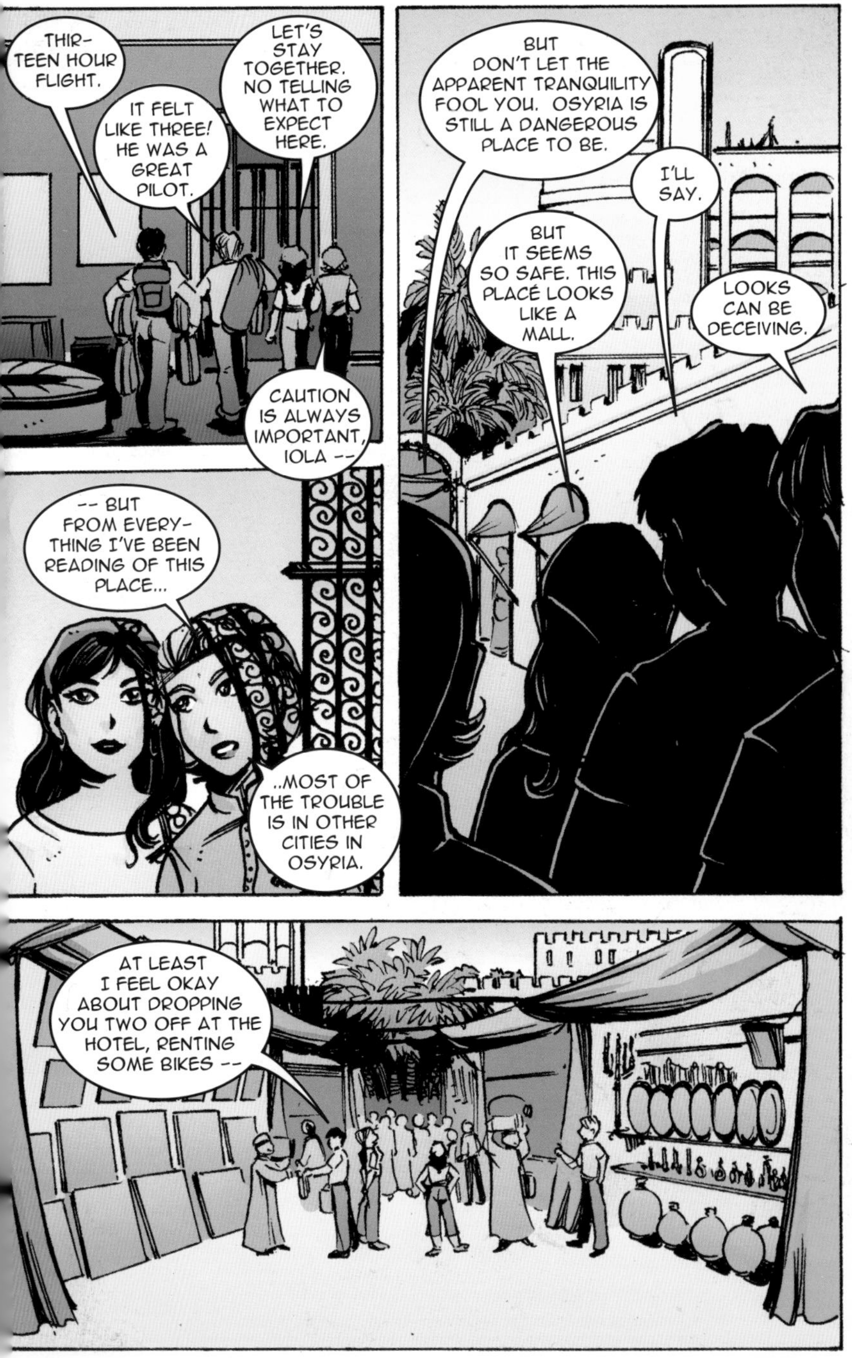
THIR-TEEN HOUR FLIGHT.
IT FELT LIKE THREE! HE WAS A GREAT PILOT.
LET'S STAY TOGETHER. NO TELLING WHAT TO EXPECT HERE.
CAUTION IS ALWAYS IMPORTANT, IOLA --
-- BUT FROM EVERY-THING I'VE BEEN READING OF THIS PLACE...
..MOST OF THE TROUBLE IS IN OTHER CITIES IN OSYRIA.
BUT DON'T LET THE APPARENT TRANQUILITY FOOL YOU. OSYRIA IS STILL A DANGEROUS PLACE TO BE.
I'LL SAY.
BUT IT SEEMS SO SAFE. THIS PLACE LOOKS LIKE A MALL.
LOOKS CAN BE DECEIVING.
AT LEAST I FEEL OKAY ABOUT DROPPING YOU TWO OFF AT THE HOTEL, RENTING SOME BIKES --

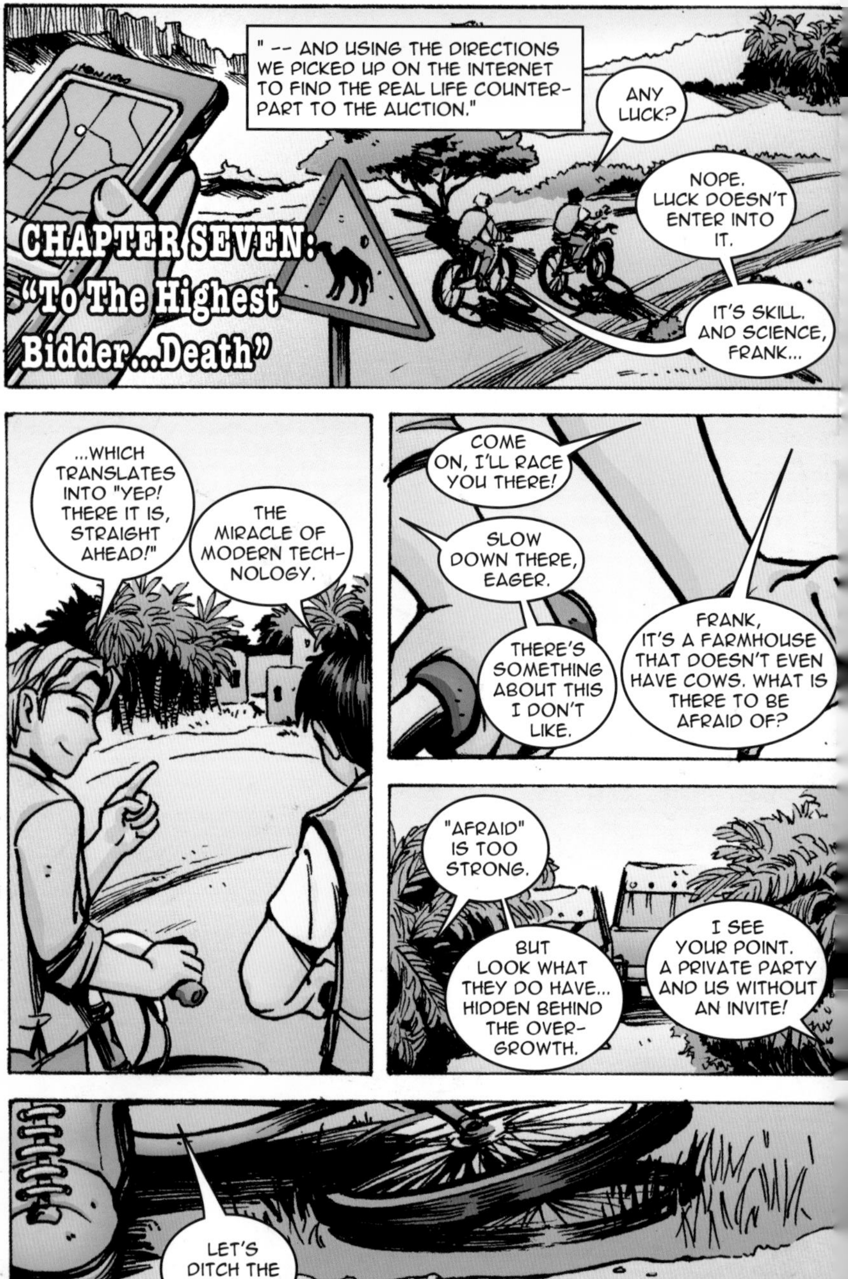
" -- AND USING THE DIRECTIONS WE PICKED UP ON THE INTERNET TO FIND THE REAL LIFE COUNTER-PART TO THE AUCTION."
CHAPTER SEVEN: "To The Highest Bidder...Death"
ANY LUCK?
NOPE. LUCK DOESN'T ENTER INTO IT.
IT'S SKILL. AND SCIENCE, FRANK...
...WHICH TRANSLATES INTO "YEP! THERE IT IS, STRAIGHT AHEAD!"
THE MIRACLE OF MODERN TECH-NOLOGY.
COME ON, I'LL RACE YOU THERE!
SLOW DOWN THERE, EAGER.
THERE'S SOMETHING ABOUT THIS I DON'T LIKE.
FRANK, IT'S A FARMHOUSE THAT DOESN'T EVEN HAVE COWS. WHAT IS THERE TO BE AFRAID OF?
"AFRAID" IS TOO STRONG.
BUT LOOK WHAT THEY DO HAVE... HIDDEN BEHIND THE OVER-GROWTH.
I SEE YOUR POINT. A PRIVATE PARTY AND US WITHOUT AN INVITE!
LET'S DITCH THE BIKES --

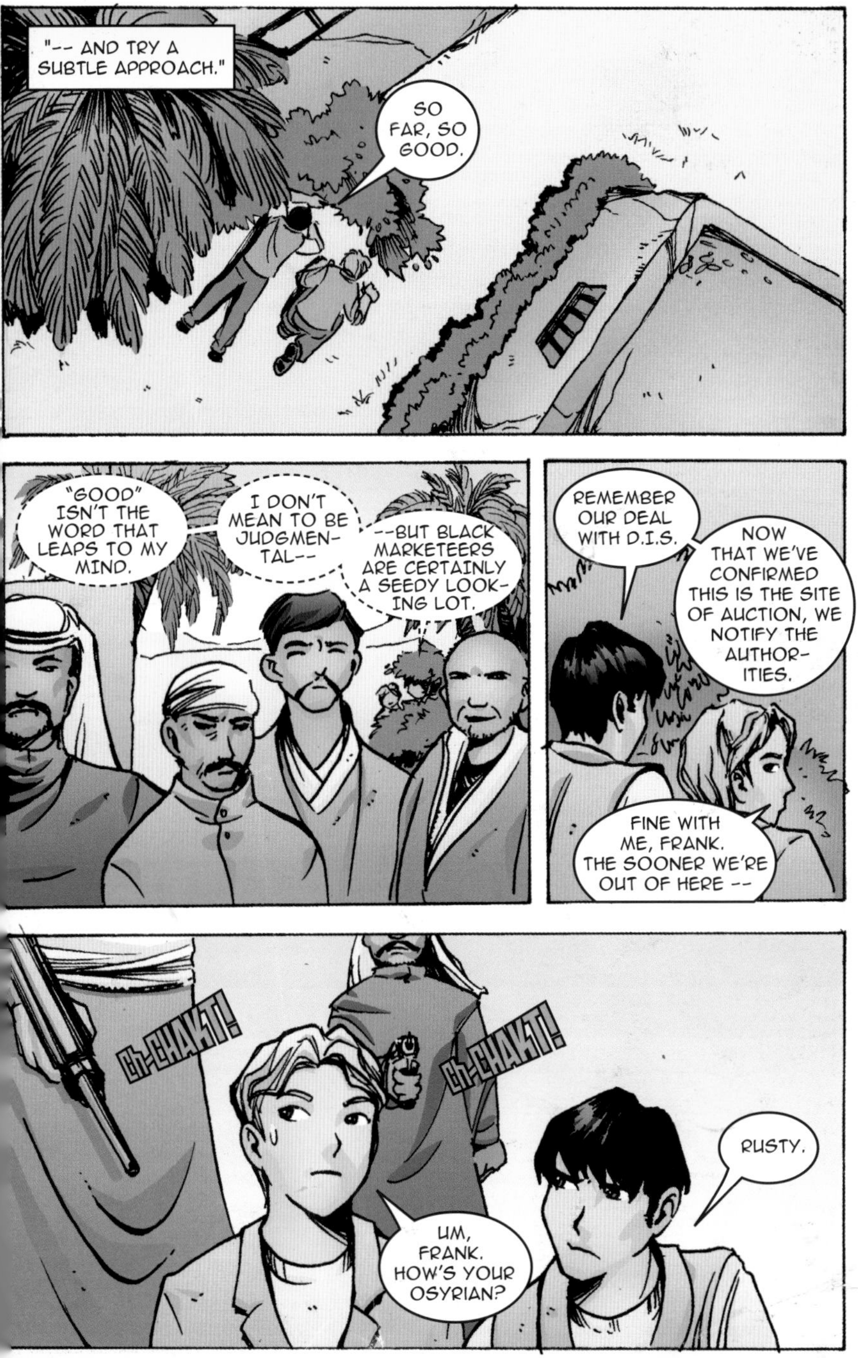
"-- AND TRY A SUBTLE APPROACH."
SO FAR, SO GOOD.
"GOOD" ISN'T THE WORD THAT LEAPS TO MY MIND.
I DON'T MEAN TO BE JUDGMENTAL--
--BUT BLACK MARKETEERS ARE CERTAINLY A SEEDY LOOKING LOT.
REMEMBER OUR DEAL WITH D.I.S.
NOW THAT WE'VE CONFIRMED THIS IS THE SITE OF AUCTION, WE NOTIFY THE AUTHORITIES.
FINE WITH ME, FRANK. THE SOONER WE'RE OUT OF HERE --
CH-CHAKT!
CH-CHAKT!
RUSTY.
UM, FRANK. HOW'S YOUR OSYRIAN?

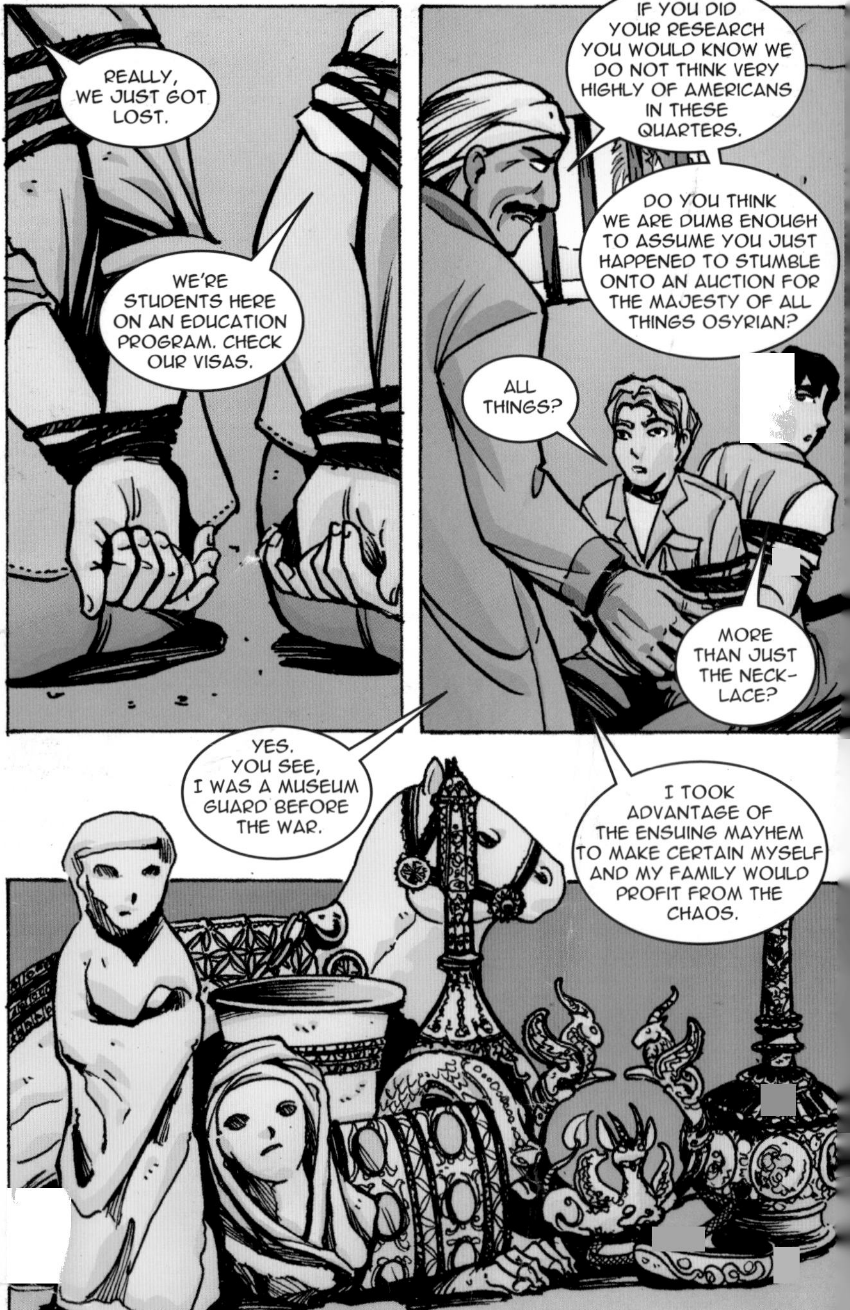

REALLY, WE JUST GOT LOST.
WE'RE STUDENTS HERE ON AN EDUCATION PROGRAM. CHECK OUR VISAS.
IF YOU DID YOUR RESEARCH YOU WOULD KNOW WE DO NOT THINK VERY HIGHLY OF AMERICANS IN THESE QUARTERS.
DO YOU THINK WE ARE DUMB ENOUGH TO ASSUME YOU JUST HAPPENED TO STUMBLE ONTO AN AUCTION FOR THE MAJESTY OF ALL THINGS OSYRIAN?
ALL THINGS?
MORE THAN JUST THE NECK-LACE?
YES. YOU SEE, I WAS A MUSEUM GUARD BEFORE THE WAR.
I TOOK ADVANTAGE OF THE ENSUING MAYHEM TO MAKE CERTAIN MYSELF AND MY FAMILY WOULD PROFIT FROM THE CHAOS.

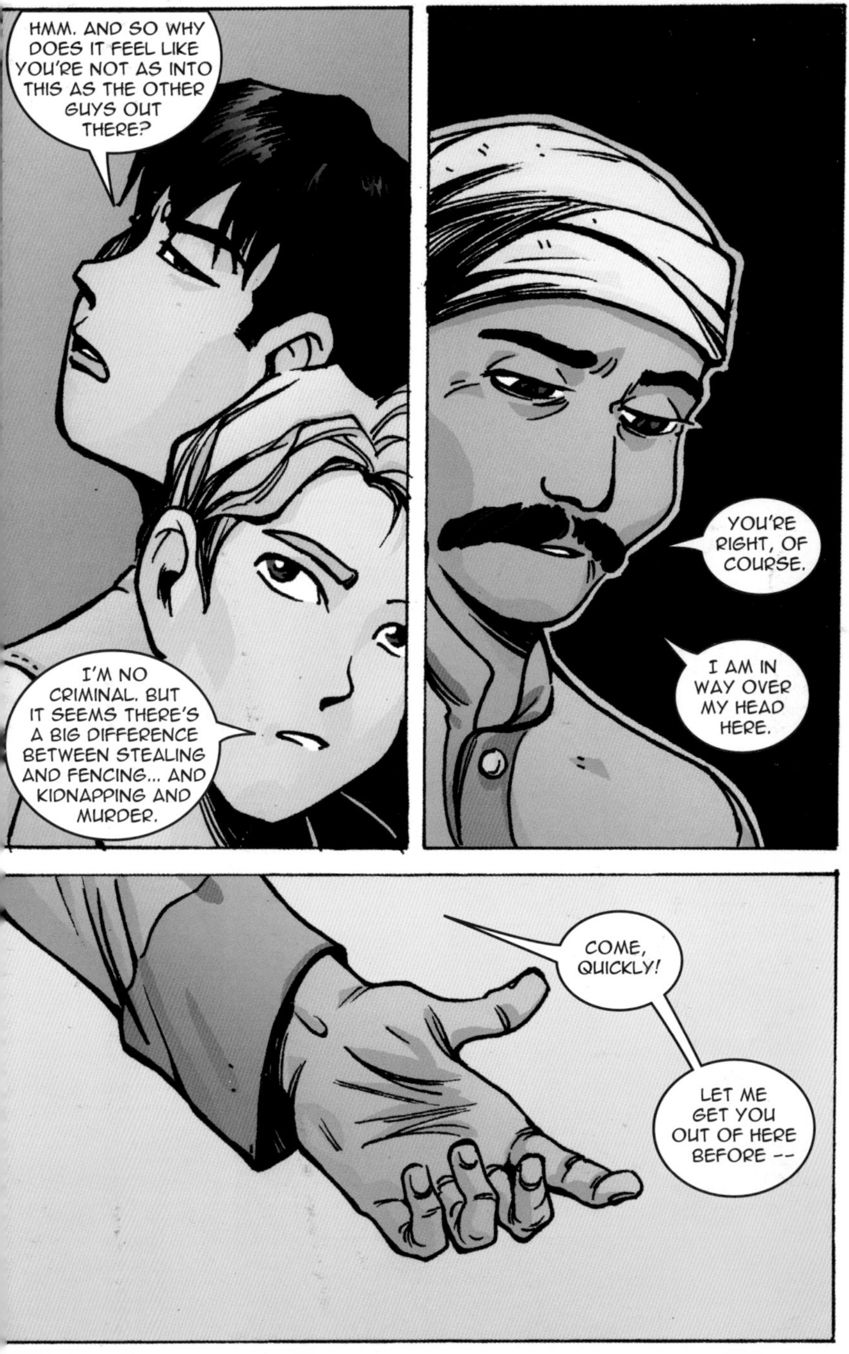
HMM. AND SO WHY DOES IT FEEL LIKE YOU'RE NOT AS INTO THIS AS THE OTHER GUYS OUT THERE?
I'M NO CRIMINAL. BUT IT SEEMS THERE'S A BIG DIFFERENCE BETWEEN STEALING AND FENCING... AND KIDNAPPING AND MURDER.
YOU'RE RIGHT, OF COURSE.
I AM IN WAY OVER MY HEAD HERE.
COME, QUICKLY!
LET ME GET YOU OUT OF HERE BEFORE --

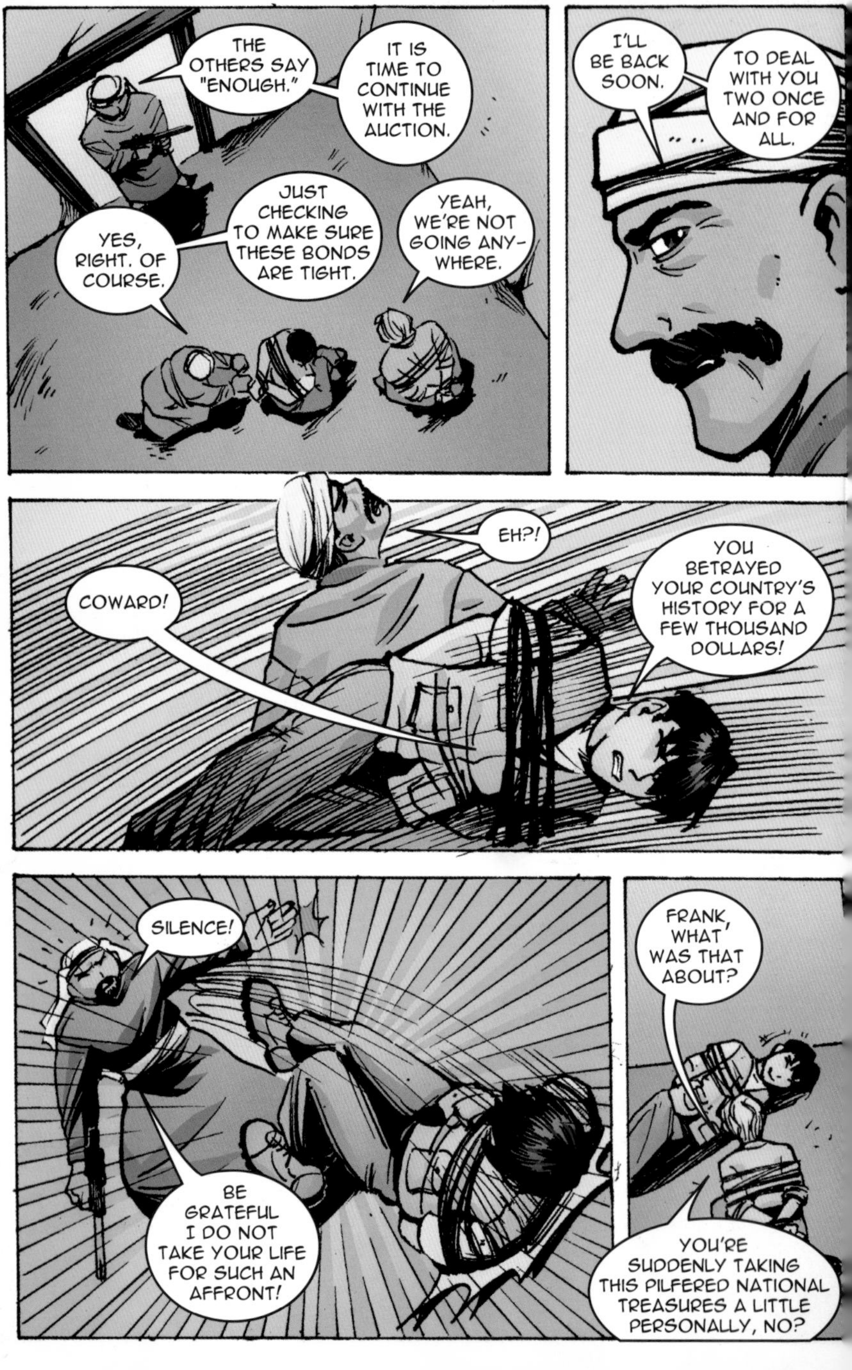
THE OTHERS SAY "ENOUGH."
IT IS TIME TO CONTINUE WITH THE AUCTION.
YES, RIGHT. OF COURSE.
JUST CHECKING TO MAKE SURE THESE BONDS ARE TIGHT.
YEAH, WE'RE NOT GOING ANY-WHERE.
I'LL BE BACK SOON.
TO DEAL WITH YOU TWO ONCE AND FOR ALL.
EH?!
COWARD!
YOU BETRAYED YOUR COUNTRY'S HISTORY FOR A FEW THOUSAND DOLLARS!
SILENCE!
BE GRATEFUL I DO NOT TAKE YOUR LIFE FOR SUCH AN AFFRONT!
FRANK, WHAT WAS THAT ABOUT?
YOU'RE SUDDENLY TAKING THIS PILFERED NATIONAL TREASURES A LITTLE PERSONALLY, NO?

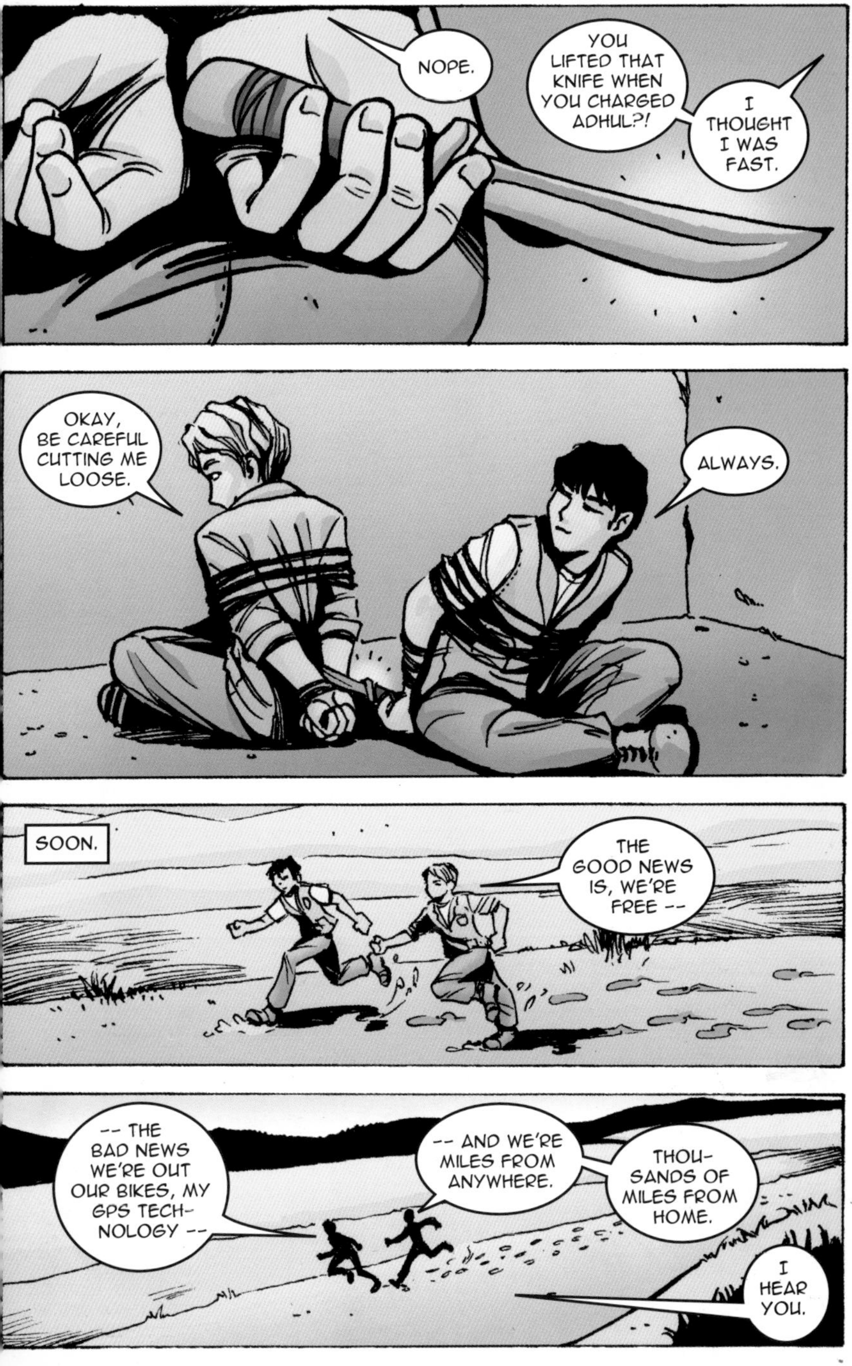
NOPE.
YOU LIFTED THAT KNIFE WHEN YOU CHARGED ADHUL?!
I THOUGHT I WAS FAST.
OKAY, BE CAREFUL CUTTING ME LOOSE.
ALWAYS.
SOON.
THE GOOD NEWS IS, WE'RE FREE --
-- THE BAD NEWS WE'RE OUT OUR BIKES, MY GPS TECH-NOLOGY --
-- AND WE'RE MILES FROM ANYWHERE.
THOU-SANDS OF MILES FROM HOME.
I HEAR YOU.

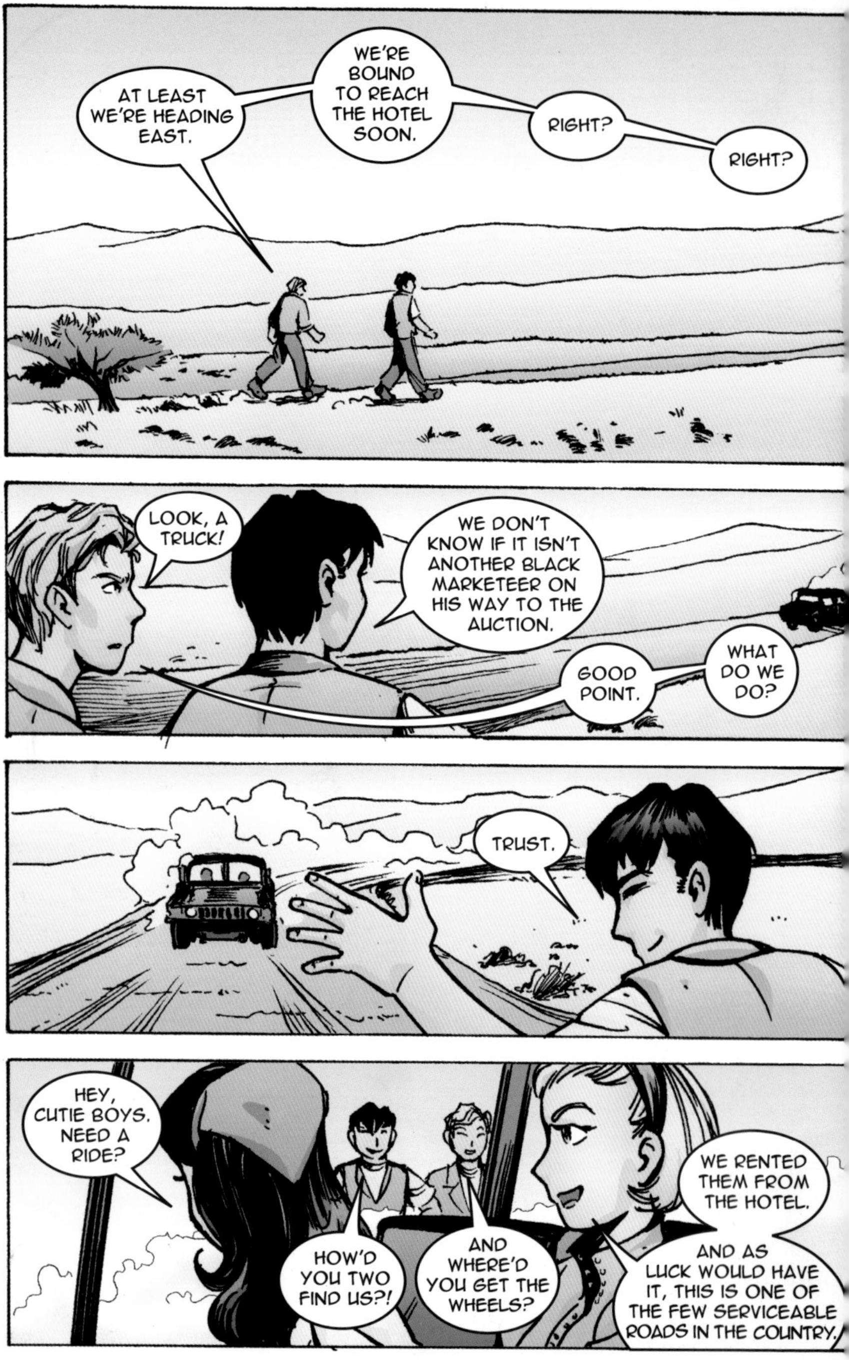
AT LEAST WE'RE HEADING EAST.
WE'RE BOUND TO REACH THE HOTEL SOON.
RIGHT?
RIGHT?
LOOK, A TRUCK!
WE DON'T KNOW IF IT ISN'T ANOTHER BLACK MARKETEER ON HIS WAY TO THE AUCTION.
GOOD POINT.
WHAT DO WE DO?
TRUST.
...
HEY, CUTIE BOYS. NEED A RIDE?
HOW'D YOU TWO FIND US?!
AND WHERE'D YOU GET THE WHEELS?
WE RENTED THEM FROM THE HOTEL.
AND AS LUCK WOULD HAVE IT, THIS IS ONE OF THE FEW SERVICEABLE ROADS IN THE COUNTRY.

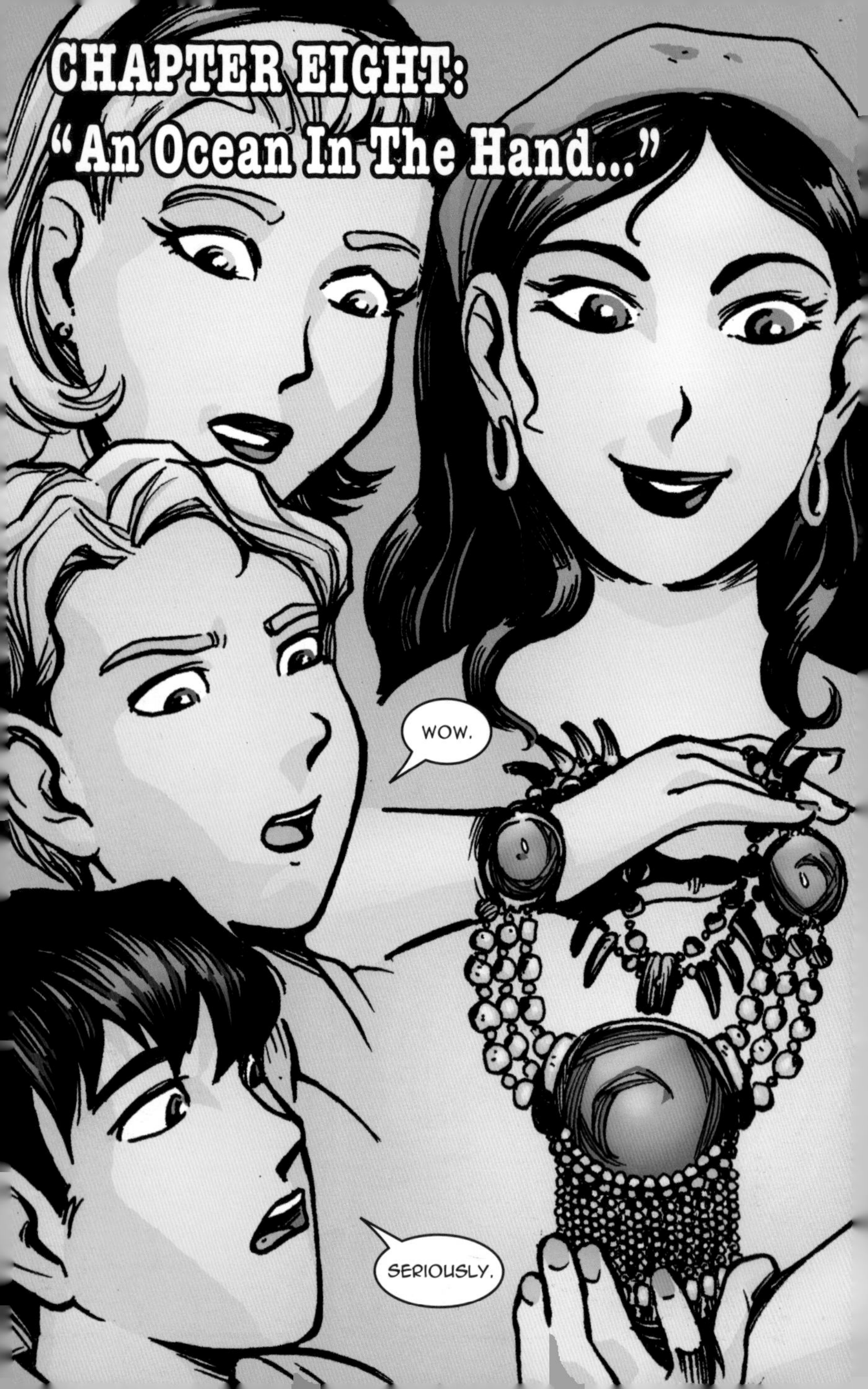
CHAPTER EIGHT:
"An Ocean In The Hand..."
WOW.
SERIOUSLY.

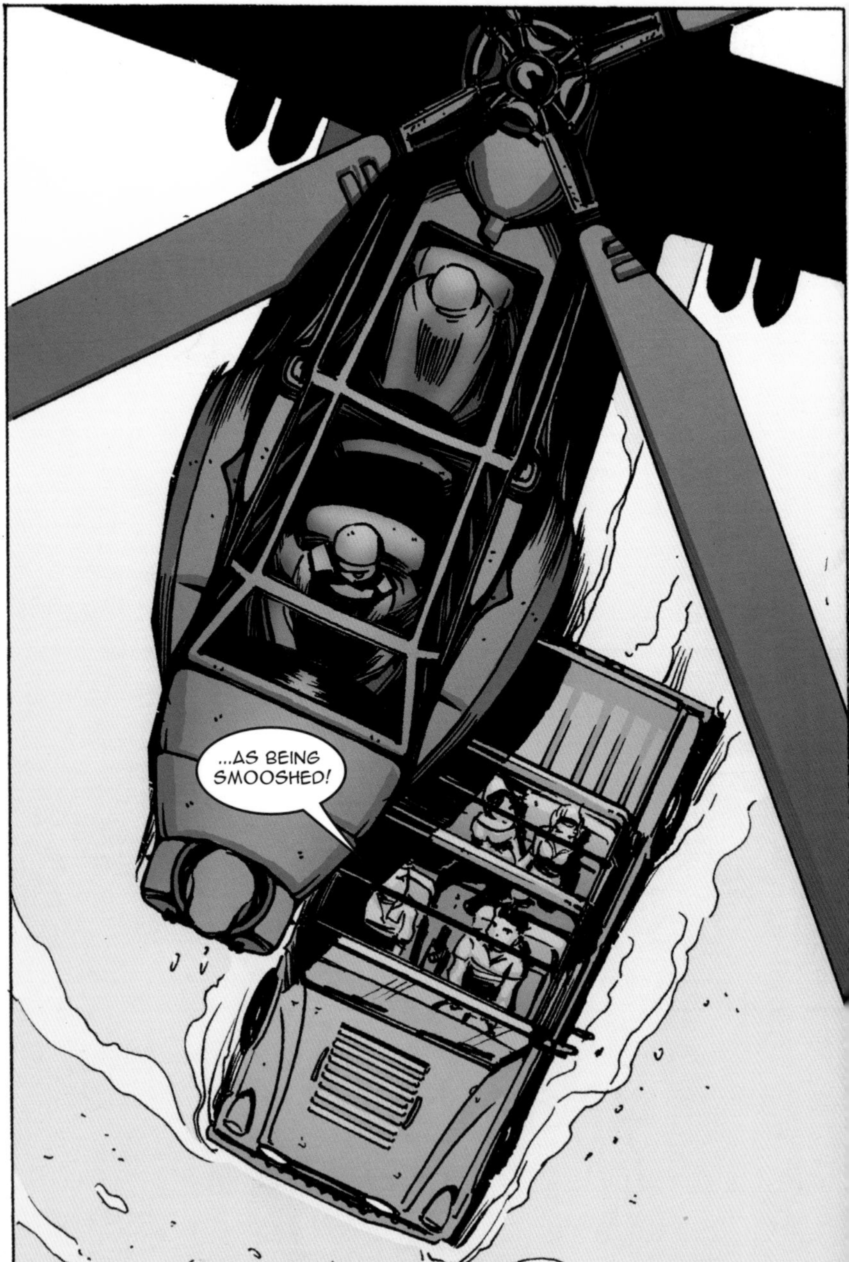
...AS BEING
SMOOSHED!

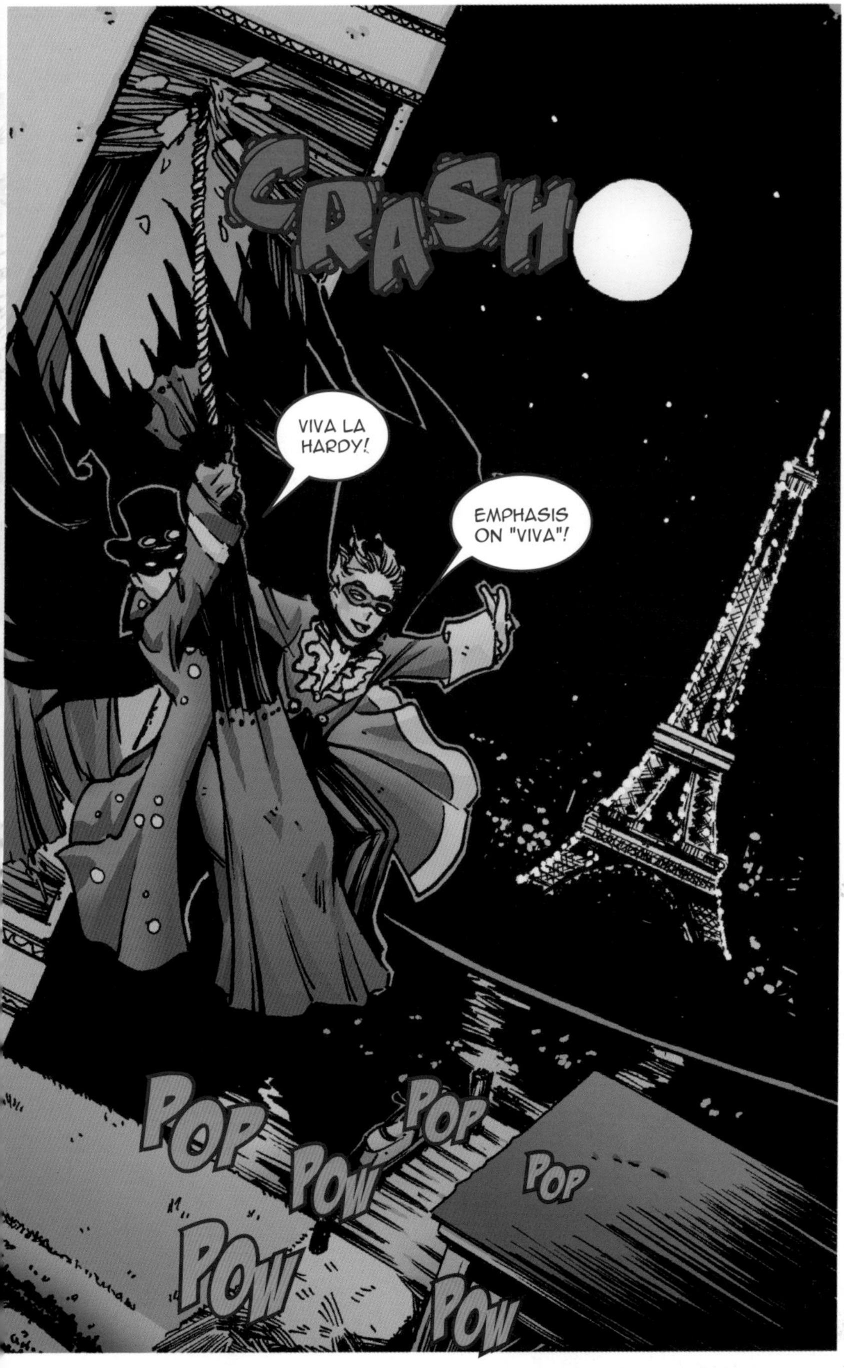
CRASH
VIVA LA HARDY!
EMPHASIS ON "VIVA"!
POP
POW
POP
POP
POW
POW

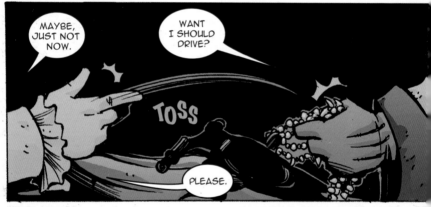

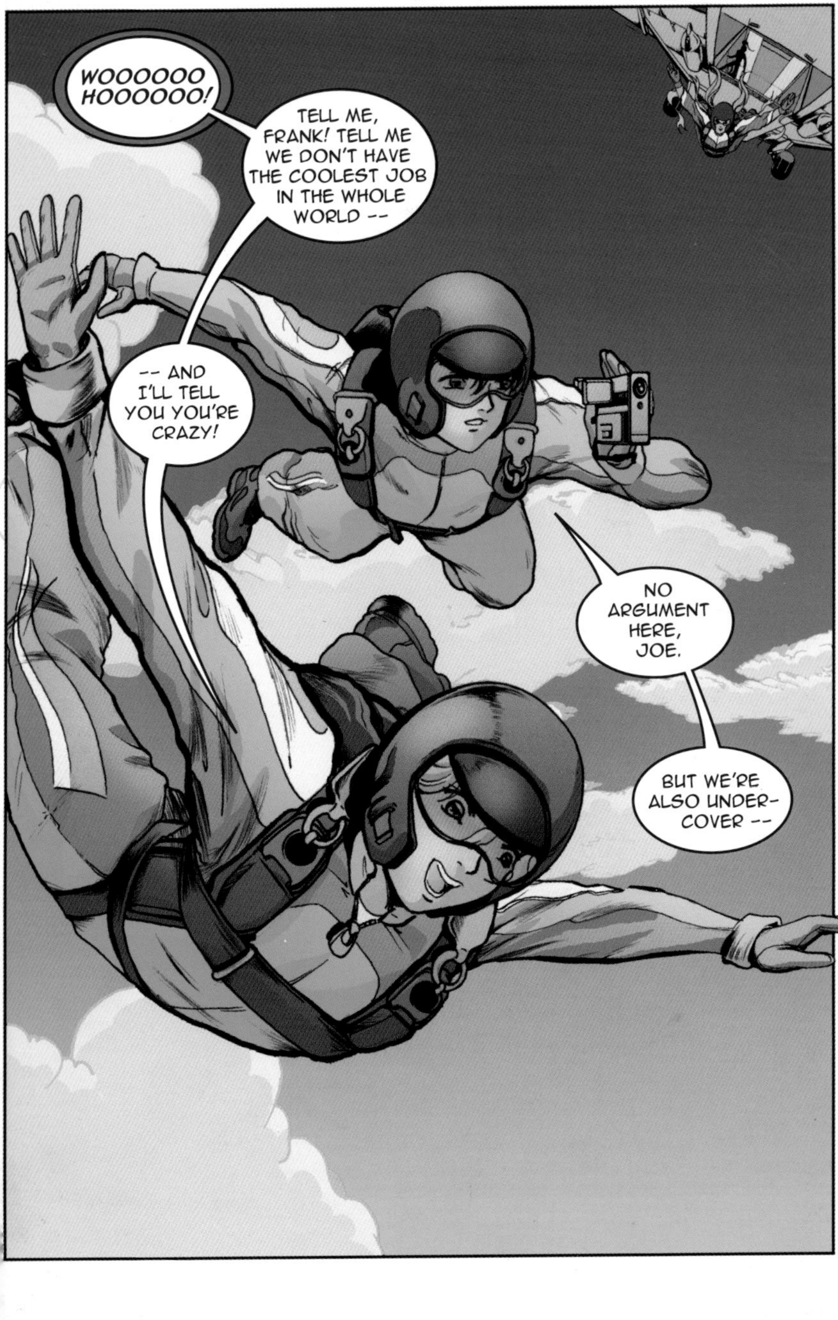
WOOOOOO HOOOOOO!
TELL ME, FRANK! TELL ME WE DON'T HAVE THE COOLEST JOB IN THE WHOLE WORLD --
-- AND I'LL TELL YOU YOU'RE CRAZY!
NO ARGUMENT HERE, JOE.
BUT WE'RE ALSO UNDER-COVER --

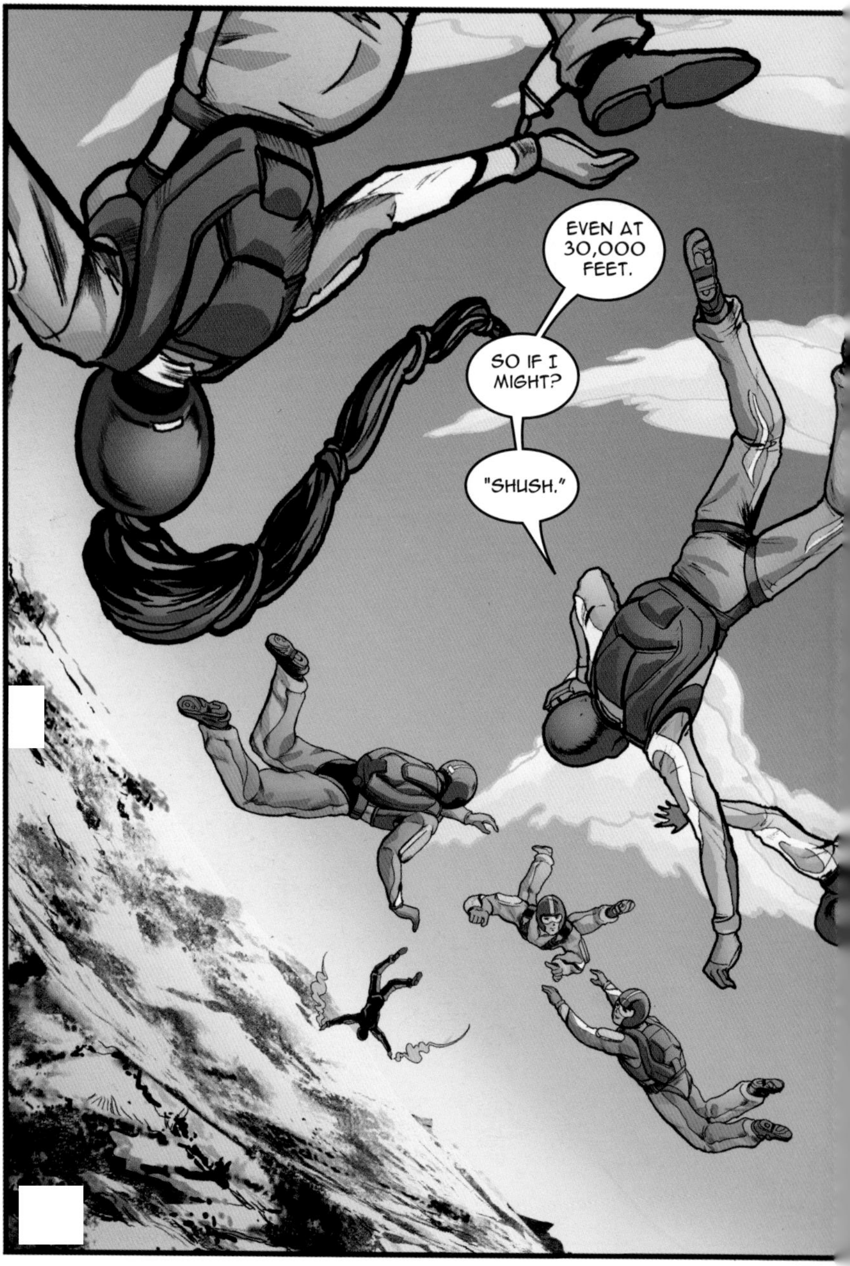
EVEN AT 30,000 FEET.
SO IF I MIGHT?
"SHUSH."

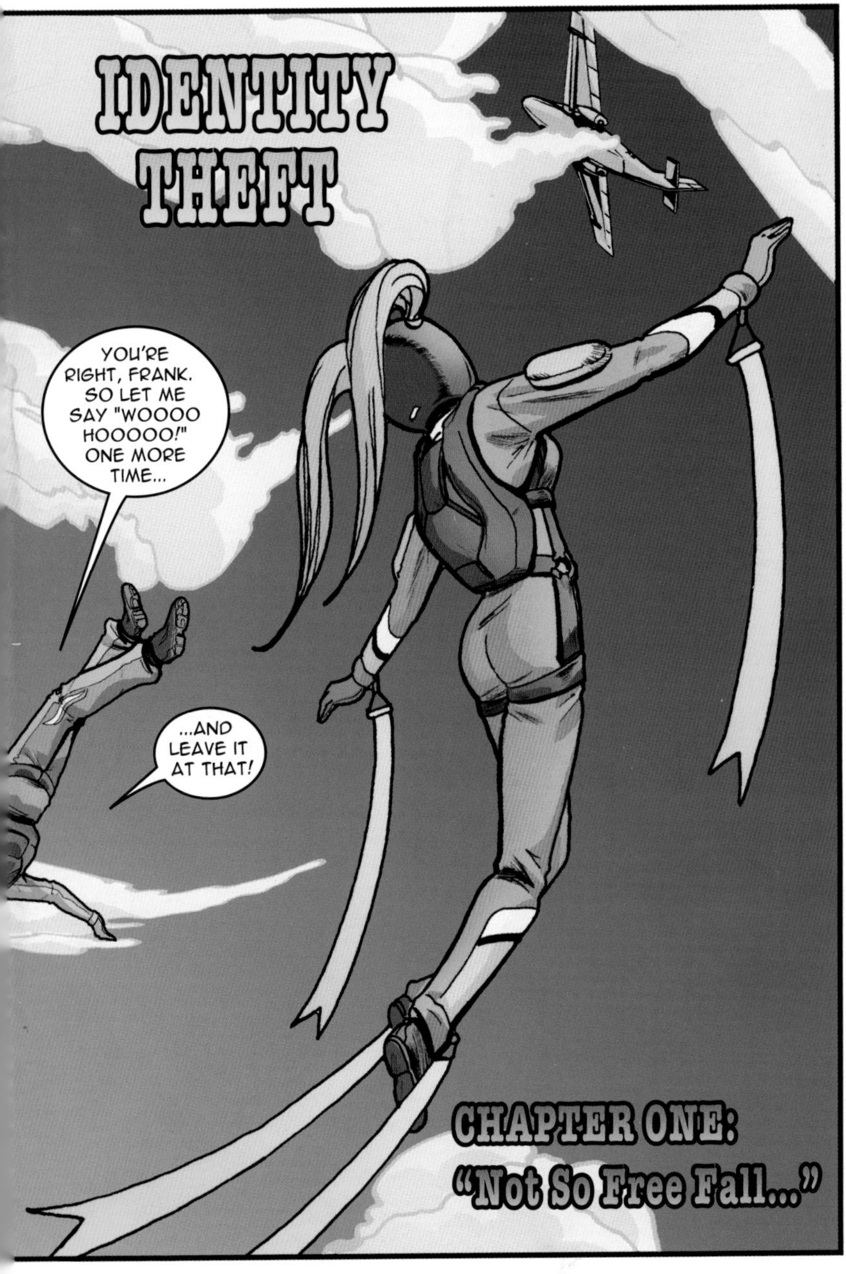
IDENTITY THEFT
YOU'RE RIGHT, FRANK. SO LET ME SAY "WOOOO HOOOOO!" ONE MORE TIME...
...AND LEAVE IT AT THAT!
CHAPTER ONE:
"Not So Free Fall..."

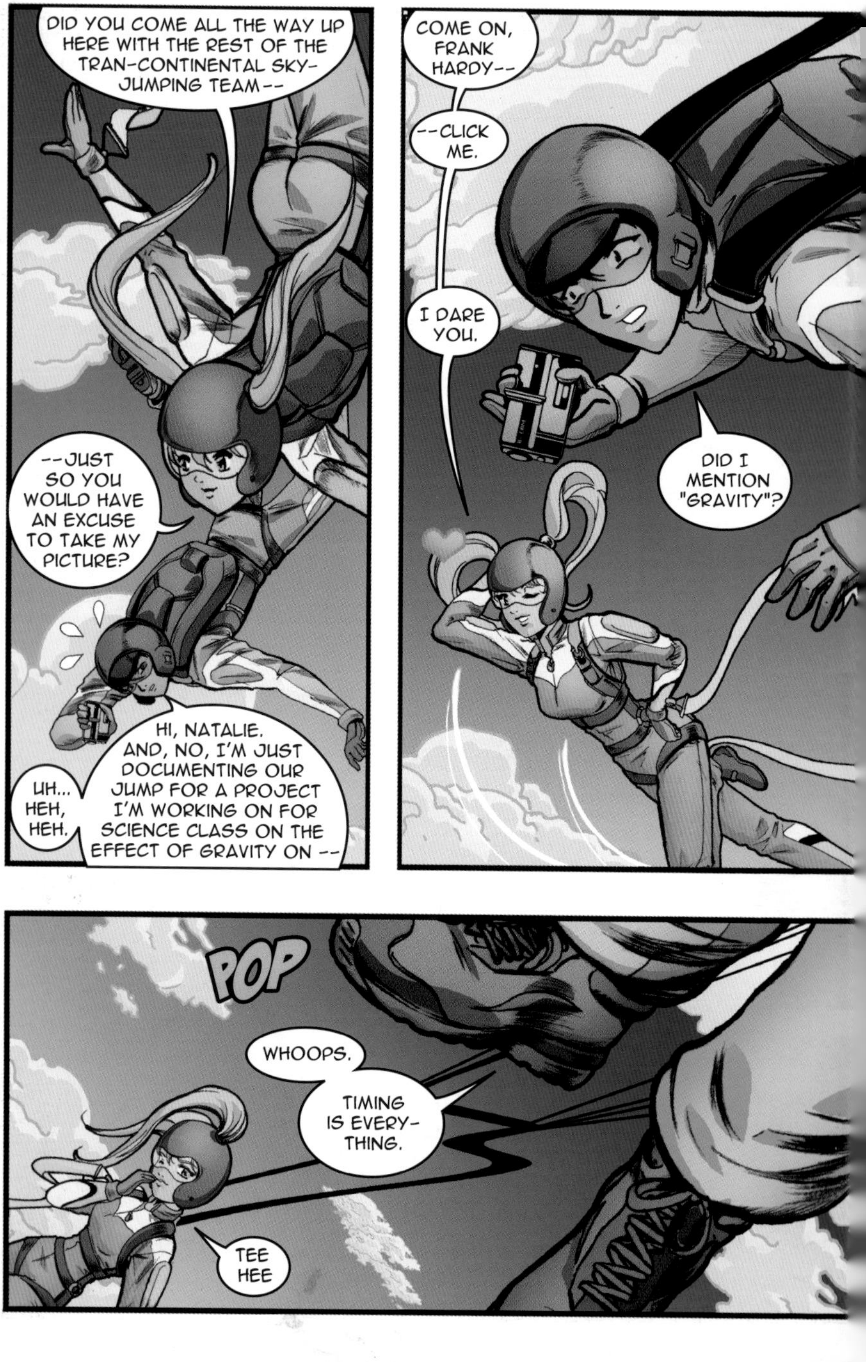
DID YOU COME ALL THE WAY UP HERE WITH THE REST OF THE TRAN-CONTINENTAL SKY-JUMPING TEAM--
--JUST SO YOU WOULD HAVE AN EXCUSE TO TAKE MY PICTURE?
UH... HEH, HEH.
HI, NATALIE. AND, NO, I'M JUST DOCUMENTING OUR JUMP FOR A PROJECT I'M WORKING ON FOR SCIENCE CLASS ON THE EFFECT OF GRAVITY ON --
COME ON, FRANK HARDY--
--CLICK ME.
I DARE YOU.
DID I MENTION "GRAVITY"?
POP
WHOOPS.
TIMING IS EVERY-THING.
TEE HEE

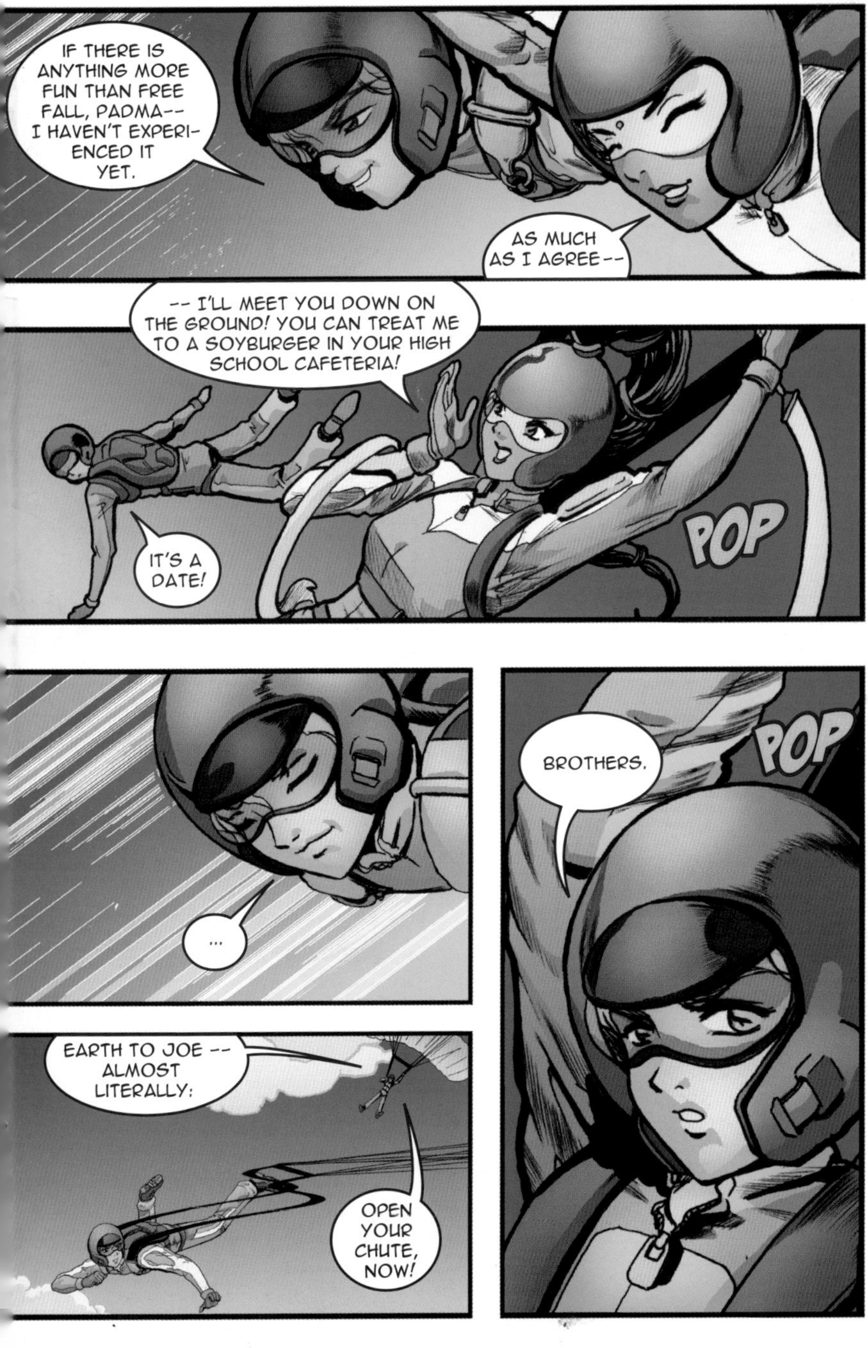
IF THERE IS ANYTHING MORE FUN THAN FREE FALL, PADMA-- I HAVEN'T EXPERIENCED IT YET.
AS MUCH AS I AGREE--
-- I'LL MEET YOU DOWN ON THE GROUND! YOU CAN TREAT ME TO A SOYBURGER IN YOUR HIGH SCHOOL CAFETERIA!
IT'S A DATE!
POP
...
BROTHERS.
POP
EARTH TO JOE -- ALMOST LITERALLY:
OPEN YOUR CHUTE, NOW!

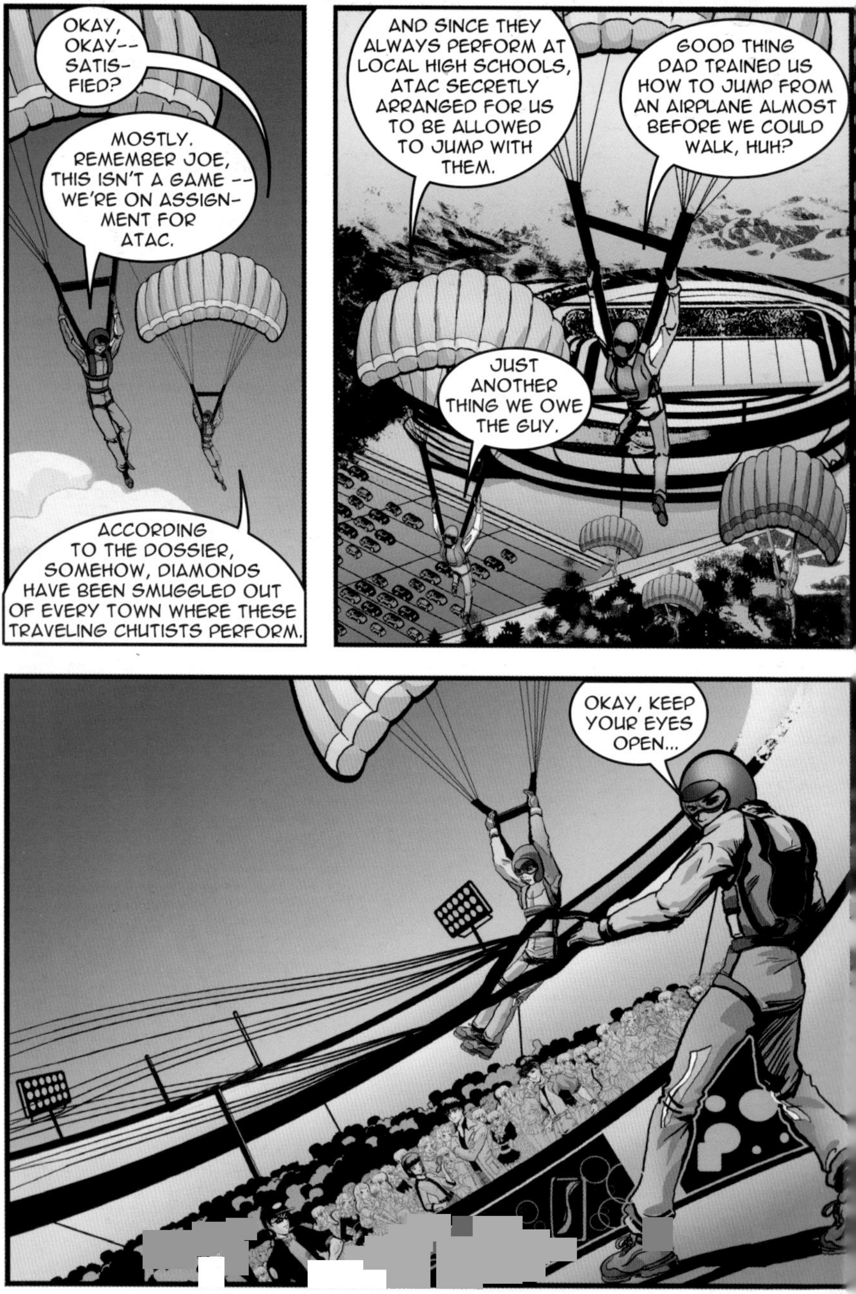
OKAY, OKAY-- SATIS-FIED?
MOSTLY. REMEMBER JOE, THIS ISN'T A GAME -- WE'RE ON ASSIGN-MENT FOR ATAC.
ACCORDING TO THE DOSSIER, SOMEHOW, DIAMONDS HAVE BEEN SMUGGLED OUT OF EVERY TOWN WHERE THESE TRAVELING CHUTISTS PERFORM.
AND SINCE THEY ALWAYS PERFORM AT LOCAL HIGH SCHOOLS, ATAC SECRETLY ARRANGED FOR US TO BE ALLOWED TO JUMP WITH THEM.
GOOD THING DAD TRAINED US HOW TO JUMP FROM AN AIRPLANE ALMOST BEFORE WE COULD WALK, HUH?
JUST ANOTHER THING WE OWE THE GUY.
OKAY, KEEP YOUR EYES OPEN...

Don't miss THE HARDY BOYS Graphic Novel #2 – "Identity Theft"